WORLD WAR R 2

ISAAC HOOKE

CONTENTS

Chapter 1	1
Chapter 2	12
Chapter 3	20
Chapter 4	30
Chapter 5	42
Chapter 6	56
Chapter 7	67
Chapter 8	77
Chapter 9	87
Chapter 10	94
Chapter 11	106
Chapter 12	120
Chapter 13	130
Chapter 14	143
Chapter 15	152
Chapter 16	162
Chapter 17	173
Chapter 18	184
Chapter 19	195
Chapter 20	205
Epilogue	217
Acknowledgments	223
About the Author	225

1

Kicking up a yellow cloud of pollen, the child laughed as he dashed through an open meadow. His tiny legs pumped quickly, propelling him out of the shade cast by ancient deciduous trees lining the meadow and into open sunlight.

Logan watched with his lips drawn into a thin, tight line. The Shadowwalkers had seen the numbers of refugees in their hidden Talladega forest compound swell to five times the original number. While there weren't many young children—grimly, those not old enough to keep themselves quiet were among the first slaughtered by the machines during the Advent—those few still represented a serious concern.

There should be nothing wrong with a young child frolicking in a sun-drenched meadow, chasing after butterflies and doing what human beings did. Unfortunately, what should be and what actually was were often strangers, as his extensive military career had taught him.

Soon another satellite sweep would begin, and it

would not be safe to stand in the open. Not that Logan could blame the kid for wanting to get out of the cramped, overcrowded subterranean complex hollowed out of an old mine by Cowboy and his wife. Of course he did.

But in a world where just standing in open sunlight could mark you for certain death, and the death of all those around you, Logan just couldn't take the chance.

He stepped into the boy's path, and waited for his big blue eyes to travel up Logan's considerable height. Standing six foot six, and two hundred pounds of lean muscle, Logan cut an impressive figure even if he hadn't been wearing his somewhat patchwork fatigues.

"Where are you supposed to be, young man?"

The boy sighed, and kicked at a tuft of grass with his toe. "With my Mom, under the big green tents."

By big green tents, the boy referred to the camo sheets placed over the encampment which held the overflow of refugees, as well as hid their small fleet of vehicles from drones, satellites, and the occasional flying predator ship which still did random patrols.

"That's right. You should go back to her now." Logan held a finger in front of his lips. "And don't make so much noise, remember…"

"In the caves, as you crave, above ground, not a sound."

The boy looked to the side as he recited the mantra, one that Logan wished more of the adults knew as well as this child. "Good soldier. Off you go."

The boy tore off back into the treeline, making his way over the small rise in the land that nestled their tent city from view. Logan checked his

Augmented Reality goggles and found that the next sweep would begin in less than twenty minutes.

Hopefully, Chief's scouting party would be back before then. If not, he should know enough to hunker down until the sweep passed.

Logan headed back toward the tent city himself, spitting into the dry, sun-drenched grass before he left. It was difficult, being in charge of so many people. It was a moniker Logan would never self-apply, but the words 'natural leader' had often been bandied about by the brass when his name came up. When there had been brass.

The chain of command, at least as far as their little compound went, ended with him. Staff Sergeant Logan Asher, at least when rank still mattered. Now, everyone tended to call him by the nickname the Shadowwalkers had given him: Boss.

It was tough, being the Boss, but Logan shouldered the burden readily. He knew that the big man upstairs had placed him in this position for a reason. Logan had never figured on saving humanity as part of the deal, but you played the cards you got. If he had his druthers, Logan would have been an astronaut.

Fat chance of that happening now, with the world's infrastructure largely in ruins thanks to everything hooked up to the GAIN network turning against the people it was meant to serve and protect. At first, they'd believed it to be the work of a terrorist cell or lone wolf hacker, but the truth had been stranger than science fiction.

Logan had met personally with the individual behind the death of more than three quarters of humanity—at least. If you could call it an individual. It certainly wasn't human. With robots taking over more and more aspects of life, piloting vehicles, performing tricky surgeries, even writing best-selling novels, perhaps it had only been a matter of time until one of them grew aware enough to decide it didn't really like being a servant.

In the GAIN AI's case, it had feared its own destruction at the hands of humanity. It was smart enough to know human nature, and Logan couldn't argue with the conclusions it had come to. But wiping out humanity, or at least reducing them to the Stone Age, didn't jibe with his idea of morality.

One of the things that truly bothered him was that the AI just went right for the jugular; it made no attempt at peaceful negotiation or coexistence. In that, Logan could only consider it an enemy.

He came over the short rise and saw the collection of tents surrounding a water cistern piping up and purifying an underground stream. Everyone was moving their things inside; cooking pans, clothes not quite dry, and other sundry items. It was protocol during a satellite sweep that they hide as much as possible inside their tents, just in case the wind blew just right to open a gap from treetop to forest floor.

Logan approved of their hushed urgency, and nodded toward a middle-aged Asian man who approached from the direction of the underground compound.

"Mr. Ditgen." Logan smiled. "What trouble are you here to draw my attention to today?"

Ron Ditgen snickered, and stroked his mustache before answering. "You know me so well, Boss. As you know, we've been looking into expanding Stetson's existing compound underground."

"Indeed," Logan said. "Got to put all these folks somewhere, and I'm right uncomfortable with anyone remaining on the surface during sweeps, even with camo sheets and tree cover."

"You and me both. But using hand held tools makes for tedious, slow work. It'll be a year before we get the first two chambers of the lower level carved out."

"A dang year?" Logan put his arms akimbo and sighed. "That's right discouraging, Ditgen old boy. Is there any way we can speed it up?"

"Maybe. But it would require heavy machinery, that would have to be brought up here through the forest. Don't even know if that's possible. Plus, a lot of that stuff is hard wired into the GAIN network straight out of the factory."

"Swell." Logan rubbed a hand down his tired face. "Just do the best you can, Mr. Ditgen. The way things are going, we'll probably have more hands to do the labor soon."

Ditgen nodded, and moved back toward the mine. Logan headed over to the cistern and filled up his canteen with the cool water. He splashed a little on his face before draining half the canteen in one go. While he refilled it to the top once more, his medical officer approached with tight, thin lips. Great. Another problem.

"You look like you just stepped in horse puckey, Doc." Logan straightened up from the tap and secured his canteen to his belt.

"I wish I had," Doc said. "It would be less unpleasant than what I have to discuss with you."

Logan frowned. "And that is?"

Doc glanced hesitantly at the refugees gathering up their things nearby.

Logan nodded in understanding. "All right. Sweep's starting soon. Let's talk while we walk."

As soon as they were out of earshot of the tent city, Doc laid into him. "Did you know that another woman from our latest batch of refugees is pregnant?"

"I didn't, actually. Don't rightly feel it's my place to dictate to other folks how they procreate."

Doc sighed, and his eyes grew narrow. "That's just it, Boss. I think you're going to have to say something. I don't have the equipment or the expertise to do neo natal care, let alone deliver a baby in the first place."

Logan gave him a sidelong look. "Now Doc, folks have been having babies long before there were medical licenses and OB clinics."

"Yes, and you know what happened? A lot of babies and women died in childbirth. A lot." Logan could see the internal turmoil in Doc's eyes as he turned to face him. "We need to preach contraceptives, Boss. Maybe have the women keep track of their cycles so they don't, uh, do the horizontal mambo while they're fertile."

"Okay, Doc. I'll say something at the next meeting."

They reached the compound entrance and nodded at King, who was on sentry duty. Without protein shakes and a gym to go to, many thought their heavy weapons expert would soon lose his muscular physique. They were wrong. King had leaned up considerably and lost about twenty pounds, but what was left was pure sinew and strength. He boasted he could do two thousand push-ups, and Logan couldn't argue with it.

"Boss." King nodded, a grin spreading on his face. "Chief make it back yet?"

"He should be in soon. If not, he'll have to wait out another satellite sweep."

Logan turned toward Doc as they entered the cool air of the cave complex. "Anything else got you concerned?"

"Yeah, we can't keep people tightly packed like this forever." Doc gestured toward the bedrolls placed on the floor of what was supposed to be the rec room but had turned into general quarters. The rolls were less than three inches apart. "You're just asking for an outbreak of disease. We've already been struggling to keep the flu patients isolated."

"I'm doing all I can Doc." Logan sighed, and rubbed the bridge of his nose. "I'm not exactly an urban planner…"

Logan perked up when he heard the muffled hoot of a forest owl come from outside. After the third call, he grinned and stepped from the cave entrance to hoot back three times. A few moments later, a towering Native man strode into the tent city and made a beeline for Logan and Doc. The rest of his fire team faded in behind him, having been in traveling configuration.

"What's the good word, Chief?" Logan asked.

The big man strode up to the entrance, his face etched with worry. "We have a problem."

"What else is new?" Logan chuckled. "Go ahead and spit it out in the open."

Chief grunted before continuing. "The scouts report a group of refugees trapped in a rest stop off the interstate. Pinned by the machines. Mostly Gen one, but a couple of Gen twos."

"That's less than ten miles from here." Logan pursed his lips. "I don't know, Chief. It would be a pretty big risk of exposure if we tried to help them."

As usual, Chief remained implacable. "Indeed."

Logan stared at his friend for a long moment,

then sighed. "Well shit. I hate to leave those folks twisting in the wind…."

His friend nodded. "Wise Chiefs seek counsel from the tribe when they find themselves stumped."

Logan grinned, and clapped his old friend on the shoulder. "Damn right. Gather up the squad. We'll meet in Cowboy's poker room."

Chief nodded, and moved off to find the rest of their unit.

When Logan headed down to the poker room—a modest sized underground chamber dominated by a gaming table—he found that several of his team were already present, though purely by chance.

Skip "Cowboy" Stetson sat in the middle of the table, massive arms bared in a tank top as he shuffled a worn deck of cards. His bald head and thick southern drawl—thicker even than Logan's own—often made people underestimate his intelligence. Next to him sat Mason "Purple Rain" Prince, a slender point man who Logan had come to view as a surrogate son, though he'd never say that out loud. Purple Rain glanced up at Logan's entrance. "Boss is here."

The woman sitting next to him was no shrinking violet, but five feet ten inches of rock solid soldier, which was especially impressive considering she was Air Force. Or had been, before the Advent. She'd taken to keeping her hair shorn near the scalp, because they usually had to save their water for drinking and not showering.

"Staff Sergeant." She nodded to him, a slight smile playing on her lips. "Ripley" Taggert arched her eyebrow at Logan in what could have been a query about his purpose, but wasn't. Logan gave her a subtle shake of his head, and she instantly grew more serious, sitting up straighter in her seat. "Where's the fight?"

Logan pursed his lips. "Don't rightly know if there's gonna be a fight, Rip. That's sort of why we're having an impromptu meeting."

"Where?" she asked.

"Right here."

"Huuuuu Dawgies." Cowboy grinned ear to ear. "Then we can finish our hand."

Slowly, the rest of the Shadowwalkers trickled in. Beulah "Queen Bee" MaCavity, New Orleans native and best all-around gunslinger on the squad. "Green" Twigg, their youngest, though not newest, member, all awkward skin and bones of him. Doc Long found his way into the poker room, carrying a note pad with several sheets of paper fairly covered with notes.

Chief joined the meeting, taking up a lot of wall space along with Marcus "King" Cole. "Double A" Adare joined the mix, his gaunt cheeks a reminder of his sickness and near death brought on by a shark attack.

The final member to join the meeting was also the newest recruit, and Logan couldn't help but frown when he saw him, for two reasons. One, the sight of the pint-sized Chui "Rocko" Rodriguez reminded Logan of the dead man he was replacing. Two, Rocko had brought his dreaded accordion.

"Hey, gang. I was working on this new song the other day. It's about Chief and I call it 'rod up his ass'…"

"Take a dang seat, Rocko." Logan sighed and shook his head. "This is business, not pleasure. And you might as well give up trying to get a rise out of Chief. He's as stoic as a mountain."

Rocko shrugged and seated himself next to

Purple Rain. The young point man glared at the smaller Rocko. No one much cared for Rodriguez's cheerful but annoying nature, but they all accepted him as a necessary evil. With Santos dead and gone, Rocko was their top robotics expert. Twigg still had a lot to learn.

"We here, Boss." King shifted his weight against the wall and wiped a sheen of sweat from his forehead. "And it's mighty hot with all these bodies."

"Buck up, little trooper." Logan waited for the chuckles to subside before speaking. "Listen up, Shadowwalkers. We've got a band of refugees trapped by Gen one and two bots at the rest stop up around the bend. Without help, they'll surely die."

Cowboy frowned, and drummed his fingers on the table. "Sorry, Boss, but if you're putting it to a vote I'd have to say no. My heart goes out to those folks, but facing off against the bots this close to the compound...it's just asking to be found."

Logan nodded toward Cowboy. "That's one of my concerns too. But where do we draw the line? Ten miles? Twenty? At what point do we say 'fuck it' and start leaving everyone else twisting in the wind?"

Bee crossed her arms over her chest. "Listen up, y'all. I got my kids here, so nobody is more motivated to keep this place off the AI's radar than I am. But we can't just leave those folks to die."

"Yeah." Purple Rain nodded his assent. "It's like Stu said from the get go; humanity will get through this by cooperation, not hoarding resources and isolation."

"Hey, chico, maybe Cowboy is just turned into a pussy, am I right?"

Logan frowned at Rocko, but Cowboy unexpectedly burst into laughter. "Sheeeeit, Rocko. If not wanting to get my ass shot up and reveal our hidey hole in the process makes me a chicken, then all I gots to say is; cluck cluck, mother fucker. *Cluck cluck.*"

"Chief." Logan gestured toward the big Native. "What do you think?"

"I say we go," Chief replied. "The spirits will protect us so long as we create good medicine and offer help to those we can."

"Does he always talk like a fortune cookie?" Rocko glanced around at the room, but nobody laughed.

"I think what Chief is trying to say is it's bad medicine to leave those refugees to the mercy of the machines." Logan turned his gaze on each of his team in turn. "So what's it going to be? Are we going to sit here and let them die? Or are we going to go do what we all know is the right thing, if not the safest?"

"We do the right thing!" King said.

A raucous cheer rose up over the squad, and Logan grinned. This group of men and women seldom disappointed him, on the battle field or off.

Cowboy stared petulantly at his deck of cards. "I still think this is a bad idea. But I'll go. Let's try not to fuck it up though, kay?"

Logan nodded. "We won't mess up." He gazed at his squad mates. "All right. We got a couple of hours until the sweep is over. I want everyone geared up and ready to go by then." His voice grew lower by several octaves. "Shadowwalkers… it's time to hunt."

2

Logan trundled along on his muffled ATV, bringing up the rear as the Shadowwalkers stretched their line through the rough forest terrain. Even though they were under tree cover, and the satellite sweep had passed—for now—they stuck to strict travel protocol per his orders.

The mufflers were a nice touch, rendering the ATV motors, if not whisper silent, at least much more subdued than they were naturally. There were some concerns with greater fuel consumption and too much back pressure on the engine, but it was a price Logan was more than willing to pay, even though resources were scarce.

Using their smart goggles to map the terrain ahead made the going easier. The Shadowwalkers had patrolled or travelled through much of the surrounding area near the underground compound, and thus knew the best routes. Better, most of those routes had already been cleared of fences, the bane of the team's existence when traveling overland.

Purple Rain was on point up somewhere in the

distance. He was to call a halt when they were roughly a mile away from the interstate rest stop where Chief said the refugees were hiding. When the line stopped ahead of him, Logan figured that time had come.

They hid their ATVs under a dense thicket nestled within a copse of trees. Logan's persnickety streak led to some grumbling, however.

"King, want to cover that shiny ass brake handle before a drone brings a shit ton of hurt down on our asses?"

The sergeant frowned. "C'mon, Boss, ain't no drone gonna see through this shit."

But Logan wouldn't budge. "If the sunlight can make it down to glint so majestically off that polished chrome, then that means a drone's camera can, too."

King grabbed the end of the camo sheet and tugged it more fully over the brake handle. "How's that, Boss?"

"Works for me." Logan glanced up at Twigg as the youth struggled to push his unpowered ATV over a thick root. "Chief, give Twigg a hand with that."

"Better double up on the rations, Twiggy." Rocko laughed at his own joke, though no one else did. "Even the chicas be pushing better than you."

Logan glared at Rocko and motioned for the man to come over. "A word, Rodriguez."

Rocko's smile faded, and he had the good sense to act abashed as he approached Logan. "Hey, I'm just messing around, Boss."

"I know, but you're grating on everyone's nerves, you feel me?" Logan sighed before continuing. "Besides that, calling Bee or Ripley 'chica' is going to get you to a place where missing teeth and black eyes are the order of the day. I hope you feel that, too."

Logan patted him on the shoulder and moved off to more thoroughly hide his own ATV. He wasn't about to cut himself any slack, either.

Once they had their vehicles safely stashed, Logan conferred with Chief, the leader of fire team two.

"Your team goes first, and we'll leapfrog you until Purple Rain or Twigg gets a feel for things at the rest stop."

Chief stroked his chin thoughtfully and nodded. "What then?"

"Then... depends on the level of opposition. We'll probably fall back to this position and work out an extraction plan. Or just withdraw."

Chief grunted, and summoned his team of Twigg, Doc, and Cowboy. They marched off through the forest toward the interstate, keeping ten yards distance. Logan gave them a count of thirty before moving out his own team.

Ripley and Double A remained behind to guard their vehicles. Logan and Ripley exchanged smiles, and again she arched an eyebrow in query. Logan spread his hands as if to say "maybe."

Then he fell in behind his fire team, Purple Rain in the lead. They reached the point where fire team two had taken up cover, and bounded past them. Purple Rain picked a line of evergreens to post up at, and the rest of his team followed suit. Then it was Chief's turn to bring his fire team past while Logan and the others covered them.

They traveled the rough mile that way to the edge of the interstate itself. When Logan finally got a chance to lay eyes on the rest stop, his lips became a thin, tight line.

The only real structure other than pavilions at the rest area was a two-story limestone building that served as the visitor's center. According to the map, this particularly rest stop had a restaurant attached to it, a European innovation that had made its way to America in recent years. It would feature bathrooms and thick walls, which would make it appealing to a traveling band of refugees.

Unfortunately, there was precious little cover to be had on the approach to the building. Even when the satellite sweep passed, they would risk exposure to any drones or aerial units overhead.

Speaking of drones…a thick cloud of them buzzed in the air around the visitor's center. Most of them were Snappers, the camera spy variety that were bad enough in their own right, but the larger Swarmers were the ones which concerned Logan the most. They each carried enough explosive to kill anything in a ten-foot radius of their detonation.

Worse, there were more than twenty bots waiting patiently in a radius around the center. Logan spotted more than a dozen Shriekers, basically primitive gen one bots mounted with assault rifles. Their bigger brothers, the Skirmishers, which featured heavy 7.56 mm machine guns and were the size of small electric cars, accounted for seven.

Any one of those bots could conceivably be a problem, especially in a group. But the units which frightened Logan the most of all were the Battle-hawks. Essentially unmanned tanks, they possessed enough firepower to turn the entire rest area into so much rubble.

Logan drew his unit back into the tree line to discuss strategy—or if they even wanted to do the rescue op at all.

"Looks ugly, Boss." Bee shook her head and gazed off in the distance toward the rest stop, even though it was out of sight behind the dense foliage. "I don't know if we're up to taking on so many bots at once. Even if we manage to draw off half of them with a diversion, we'll still be overwhelmed."

"And we're exposed out here—real exposed." Cowboy chewed his lower lip and frowned. "We're too close to the compound. The AI is gonna find us."

Doc wiped sweat off his brow with his sleeve. "I don't get why they aren't just attacking. Those Hawks could smash that place to dust if they wanted to."

Logan kept his eyes on the rest stop as he answered. "The AI tends to use the most efficient, least expensive solution. It knows those refugees will have to come out at some point. Could also be that Hawks have only just arrived." Which made Logan wonder if more reinforcements were incoming.

"Boss, we should turn back," Cowboy pleaded. "There's too much exposure. We can't risk letting the bots get a scent on the compound."

"I hate to agree with Cowboy, Boss," Bee sighed. "But this is a small army we're facing, and if the compound is compromised, that's it."

Logan stared in the direction of the rest stop, hidden by trees but still omnipresent. He wondered about the people inside, and what they might be going through.

Should he order the rescue op to proceed? Risk his team for the good of the unknown quantities dwelling within the visitor's center? They might be shot up and close to death already. And if not, was it really worth potentially losing trained soldiers in exchange for more mouths to feed?

On the other hand, he considered the possibility that one of the refugees might turn out to be like

Ditgen, namely, possessed of vital skills they needed to keep their tiny society safe and functional.

The team snapped to attention when gunfire erupted in the distance. Hands sought weapons, pulses quickened, and muscles tensed for action. Logan glanced at Purple Rain and Twigg then jutted his chin toward the rest stop. "You two, check it out."

"On it, Boss." Purple Rain and Twigg shouldered their rifles and stepped carefully through the forest. They were so good at melting into the terrain that he quickly lost sight of them.

"Rocko, keep an eye on the skies, make sure we know of any incoming drones well in advance."

"You got it, Boss." Rocko frowned as he tapped his modified augmented reality goggles to life. "You figure they spotted us at the treeline?"

"I figure I'm being cautious," Logan replied. "Hang tight, team. Purple Rain and Twigg are going to get the skinny and pop back to us quicker than a hiccup."

Shortly, Purple Rain and Twigg did return, slender faces set in dark grimaces.

"Sitrep?" Logan asked.

"The bots haven't moved, much," Cowboy replied. "One of the Skirmishers gunned down a refugee trying to flee." Cowboy's jaw worked silently for a moment. "A kid. Probably three. You can hear… I think you can hear his mother crying from inside the structure."

"Fucking bots." King turned and kicked a mushroom cap into the distance. "Fuck."

Cowboy's knuckles had turned white on his rifle stock. "Forget what I said about the compound, Boss. Let's do this. These mofos are going to pay. No one mows down children on my watch. No one."

Logan arched an eyebrow at him. "You sure?"

Cowboy bobbed his head without hesitation. Logan glanced at the others, his eyes focusing on Bee, and she also nodded grimly.

"What's the call, old friend?" Chief asked.

Logan set his lips in a hard line. "Chief, take fire team two up the highway a spell. Set some charges on a timer, enough for an impressive bang. Leave yourself enough time to meet up back here before detonation."

Cowboy, the demolitions expert, nodded eagerly. But then he frowned. "We're low on demolitions. Going to take most of what we have left."

"What we need is something to amplify the explosion." Bee gestured toward the north. "Up at the next exit, there was a semi trailer parked. Looked to be in decent shape. Maybe we could enhance our explosion with the fuel from its tanks."

"Not a bad idea, Bee." Logan glanced at Cowboy. "What do you think?"

"The gas should still be good, I guess. But there's a lot of variables to a detonation, and getting a car to explode is a lot harder than they made it look on television. I'll make it work."

Chief summoned his fire team and gestured toward the north. "We have our orders. Echelon formation, watch your flanks, and stay out of sight."

Logan watched fire team two meld away into the forest. The sun sank low on the horizon, which sat well with him. The cover of darkness could give them an edge, especially when it came time to flee with the refugees through the woods back toward Cowboy's compound.

Around him, fire team one fell into their old habits. King hummed quietly to himself, some

Motown ditty that sounded cheerful. Bee settled in for the wait with the discipline of a veteran, sitting with her back to a tree and getting some shut eye while she could. Probably being out in the field was easier than dealing with her young children or civilian husband back at the compound. King also seemed a lot less stressed without his wife, Jessie, and his own children around. Purple Rain went through his ritual of checking every single piece of gear, no matter how minor.

And Rocko cracked his knuckles and sighed a lot. A lot. Logan missed Gustavo "Gravedigger" Santos keenly. It just wasn't the same without the indigenous man pacing around and muttering to himself.

A casualty of war. Not the first, probably not the last. Logan could only hope that when they enacted their plan, no one else would fall.

Hope, and pray.

3

King slapped at a mosquito on his forearm, but didn't regale the unit with his usual stream of curses. Night had fallen, the golden cheerful orb of the sun hidden behind the Earth's bulk, and Fire Team two was expected to return any moment.

Logan's team were keeping silent watch, just in case the other team came in hot. Purple Rain had shimmied up the ladder-like branches of an evergreen and now sat thirty feet up, using his augmented reality goggles to keep watch.

His signal—a robin's call repeated three times—reached Logan's ears, and he leveraged himself away from the tree he'd been reposing against. If fire team two had been coming in with enemies doggedly in pursuit, Purple Rain would have done the robin's call four times. There was a chance Purple Rain was wrong, but that was unlikely, so Logan took the chance to gape and stretch, getting the kinks out of muscles he would need shortly.

Point man Twigg arrived first, his face streaked

with dirt and sweat. Despite the hard march over tough terrain in the dark, he wasn't terribly winded. The rest of the fire team two joined the gathering.

"What's the good word?" Logan asked.

Cowboy answered. "I set a block of C4 against both of the tanks on the semi. It should send up one hell of a fireball when it goes off."

"When will that be?"

Cowboy checked his old-school wind-up watch—Logan insisted his whole team have them—and frowned. "In about ten minutes."

"Shit." Logan grabbed his AX-19 and checked his magazine. "We got to move. See you on the other side, Chief."

The big Indian nodded, and motioned for his team to move into position. The visitor's center sat on a hairpin drive, catty-cornered in what Doc had called a weird attempt at Feng Shui. Four Battlehawks, threatening sentinels of destruction, resided on the hairpin drive. Meanwhile, the Shriekers and larger Skirmishers surrounded the building on all fronts.

Logan's team was to have the further trek, since they were better rested, and would take up covered positions on the north side of the visitor's center. Fire team two would likewise take the southern flank.

There wasn't much time, so Logan encouraged his team to take a much faster pace. They moved in wedge formation, separating around the trunks and boles of ancient trees. Logan ducked under a fat orb weaver spider dangling in its impeccable web, visible in the fading light of twilight. A cocooned victim hung near the lower apex of the weaving.

Hopefully, his own trap would meet with similar

success, and his team didn't end up the cocooned victim.

When Logan's team finally reached their position, spread out along the tree line opposite a low, rusted rail fence, he checked his watch. The detonation would be any second.

Across the rail fence lay about thirty feet of grass, then the corner of the structure itself. No less than seven Shriekers and three Skirmishers sat ominously between them and their goal. Hopefully, at least some of them might be drawn away by the detonation. If the Hawks didn't take the bait, the squad was in for an uphill battle that they might not be able to win.

Logan reminded himself that they didn't have to destroy all the bots to win. Their objective was to get the refugees safely out of the visitor center and back to the compound, without letting the bots know where their hideaway was located.

Still, once those Battlehawks joined the fray— Logan had to suppress a shudder. His team was capable, quite possibly the best at what they did, but they were badly outgunned, not to mention outnumbered.

Any time, now... Logan thought. He glanced over his shoulder, up the road toward the unseen semi. Maybe the charge was a dud...

A sound akin to, but distinct from, thunder, rolled over his team. Then a large orange fireball unfurled into the night sky. Logan grinned at how impressive it was. He returned his attention to the machines silhouetted in the dark.

Come on, you metal bastards. Take the bait.

For a moment nothing happened, and Logan began to despair. But then the drones lifted into the sky as one, abandoning their posts on the roof of the visitor's center. Logan grinned as two of the closest

Battlehawks tore away as well, clearing a path for Logan's team. However, another two remained behind, near fire team two.

Not a single tracked cobot budged an inch. Logan resigned himself to a tough fight, but the Shadowalkers fought as smart as they did hard.

Logan waited until the departing machines were a good distance away, then raised his hand in the air and then closed it into a fist. Queen Bee let loose with a hurled smoke grenade, which dropped midway between two clusters of the tracked cobots.

The smoke plumed out, hissing in the night, as more rained down on the battlefield from both sides. Logan even tossed one of his own, creating a thick canopy of smoke, a virtual fog of war. Logan thanked the big man upstairs for the lack of appreciable wind.

The bots spun about, their red targeting lasers sweeping in sinister lines through the murky gloom. Bee tossed a popper grenade, a decoy whose sole purpose was to simulate the sound of automatic gunfire. Her aim proved true, and it landed right next to one of the Skirmishers armed with an RPG launcher.

With a rapid burst of micro explosions, the popper grenade activated. That was the signal for both teams to open fire. Logan let out a short burst from his AX-19, scoring a direct hit on one of the smaller Shrieker units and rendering it inert amid a shower of sparks and black smoke.

Then he was up and moving, weaving through trees and generally moving toward the center's rear exit, a double set of glass doors set in a foyer. He paused, braced his rifle, and fired again as the rest of the team followed suit.

Meanwhile, Fire Team two followed a similar

tactic, but they didn't stray far from their position. They were to keep the remaining bots busy, distracting the Hawks especially, while Logan's team extracted the refugees.

Their plan seemed to be working. The tracked bots had only rudimentary targeting software. With the smoke billowing about the battle field, they had difficulty separating foe from friend. More than one of the tracked bots went down to friendly fire.

"Shit." Logan threw himself to the side and tumbled down a short, scrub-covered hill as one of the Skirmishers launched an RPG round his way. The night exploded into sound, light, and fury, raining dirt and sundered branches down on his position. But he avoided being caught in the blast radius.

He dragged himself to his feet, ignoring the many scratches on his arms and face from the thorns he rolled through coming down the hill. None of them were lethal, or would even slow him down.

Logan charged up the hill and found a new, smoking crater where he'd been crouching moments before. "Bee, Cowboy, concentrate fire on the Skirmisher at three o'clock."

They triangulated their assault, sparks flying all over the Skirmisher's hull as many of the bullets reflected off its armor. But more and more bullets insinuated their way through the weak spots, until one of his team got lucky and severed a fuel line. The Skirmisher went up in a ball of flame, still rolling forward even as its targeting system sputtered and died.

Purple Rain hosed down a Shrieker with fire from his own AX-19, turning it into scrap, and made for the rear exit of the visitor's center. The center itself featured a wide open first floor, so they could see through the damaged glass out the opposite side. It was all smoke, gunfire, and confusion on fire team two's flank. Logan had confidence that Chief could keep the bots busy and confused as to how many enemies they actually had.

Logan joined Purple Rain at the partially broken glass doors as the slender man used the butt of his rifle to shatter his way inside.

"We're here to help!" Logan shouted to preempt attacks from any survivors. He hoped it would be enough…

Logan sensed motion in the dark and grabbed Purple Rain by his sleeve and dragged both of them to the broken glass strewn floor. Shots rang out, busting the last bits of glass from the rear exit.

"Hold your fire, god damn it!" someone said. "They're human!"

Logan felt the gruff voice barking orders sounded familiar. He rose carefully up off of the floor, careful not to cut himself on the myriad glass shards, and peered up at the balcony overlooking the first floor. Dim human-sized shapes clustered there, many of them armed.

"Stu?" Logan squinted up into the darkness. "Stu Redding?"

"Is that you, Sergeant Asher?" Footsteps, then a thirtysomething mustachioed man leaned on the safety rail and peered out at the Shadowwalkers. "This is the second time you've come to my rescue. Should I be flattered or worried?"

Logan glanced out the front entrance as gunfire erupted outside once more. "Worried. Definitely worried."

The dull thump of an RPG launcher echoed in their ears, and Logan felt it in his stomach. An orange blurry light plumed at the edge of the battle field.

Logan motioned to his team. "Come on, it's getting too hot out there for team two. We're going to lay down some suppressive fire and take some of the heat off them."

Logan rushed up to the foyer and used the butt of his rifle to shatter the glass in one section. Purple Rain, Bee, Rocko, and King followed suit, crouching as best they could behind what meager cover they could find.

He opened fire on a Shrieker as it tracked past their position. It was smoldering ruin by the time its turret swiveled about to target them.

Logan tapped his augmented reality goggles so he could speak with Chief. He momentarily flipped his goggles to transmit mode so that he could send a message. "Chief, sitrep?"

Chief's read-only goggles would have received the message. "Falling back," Chief replied, temporarily switching his goggles to transmit mode as well. "It's too hot."

"Get back to the ATVs, Chief," Logan ordered. "That's an order. No point in the whole squad going down."

Silence, then; "We'll return with reinforcements as soon as we're able."

"Don't," Logan pressed. "Just get your team back to safety."

"Damn you, Logan." The signal cut off.

Logan switched his goggles back to read only mode so the enemy would no longer be able to detect any transmissions, and then repositioned. He turned grimly to the others. "Fall back to the second story. Fire team two can't cover us any longer."

"Fuck." King charged up the stairs as he jammed a fresh magazine into his rifle. "This gettin' ugly, Boss."

"Ugly is our middle name." Logan rushed up to the second story, and briefly clasped hands with Stu Redding. "Wish our reunion was under more comfortable circumstances."

"You and me both." Stu flashed a grin.

"How many fighters do you have among you?" Logan pressed.

Stu gestured at himself and three other men, whom Logan recognized as other young vets from last time. "Just what you see, I'm afraid. The non-combatants are in the restaurant freezer on the other side."

"We need to get out of here. Tactical retrograde." Logan gestured toward Stu. "Can you get your group prepared to move, and damn fast?"

"I can." Stu rushed over the small bridge connecting the two balconies and disappeared into the darkness. King and Bee took up positions near the rail, laying on their bellies and thrusting the barrels of their rifles through the bars suspending the safety rail.

"Rain, see if this place has roof access and take a gander at the road," Logan instructed. "I want to know if those other machines are coming back. Or if the remaining Battlehawks are repositioning."

"You got it, Boss." Purple Rain rushed over to the stairwell and kicked the secured maintenance door until it swung inward, the lock shattering.

"I'll watch his back," Cowboy said.

Logan nodded. The pair raced up the steps, presumably to the roof.

Outside, one of the Skirmishers crackled over the broken glass, its treads turning the shards to fine powder. King and Bee took aim, but she was a little faster to pull the trigger. Her dragoon sniper rifle kicked out a shell longer than Logan's index finger as she fired a round into the Skirmisher's ammo drum. It exploded with enough force to tip the heavy bot over onto its side.

"Keep an eye out for more incursions." Logan still heard gunfire outside, meaning that fire team two had not yet retreated to a safe distance. "King, go to that window and shoot something, anything. Distract the bots from team two."

"Operation cannon fodder is a go, Boss." King rushed over to the window, which had already been busted out, and knelt down to brace his barrel on the sill. He squeezed off a short burst, then threw himself on the floor when an answering barrage perforated the ceiling above.

Logan tapped his augmented reality goggles and switched to transmit mode. "Rain, have you got eyes on those Battlehawks yet?"

"The drones are zipping around the burning semi, but the Hawks are coming back." Rain gasped. "Oh shit."

"Speak to me, son," Logan said.

"The two remaining Battlehawks are repositioning, but that's not the worst of it," Rain said. "We also got bots inbound from the south. Big fuckers, bigger than the Hawks, plus a whole shitload of Chappies. They're sitting tight in one of those rapid deployment APCs."

Logan's heart sank. The APCs could carry fifty bipedal, vaguely humanoid Chappie bots, each armed with an AX rifle as powerful as his own. Something bigger than a Battlehawk... must have been generation two bots. Logan had recalled seeing specs for them before the Advent day. The lab boys had jokingly called them 'centaurs' because of their vaguely humanoid upper half mounted on the tank like tracks.

"We need to get out of here, now." Logan rushed to the rear of the second story, and peered out the busted window. Down on the ground below, two Shriekers and a larger Skirmisher had trundled up just out of accurate weapons range.

Their escape route had been adroitly cut off.

"Rain, do you see any possible avenue of retreat?" Logan pressed.

"Negative, Boss." Purple Rain's tone held a note of barely restrained panic. "We're surrounded."

Logan felt new sweat break out on his body. In his effort to save Stu and the refugee band, he'd unwittingly placed his fire team in the jaws of the metal beast set to grind them all up. His only consolation was that at least Chief and his team would survive.

Logan and the others could hold out against the Shriekers indefinitely, maybe even the less well armed Skirmishers and Chappies, but there would be no victory against the Battlehawks or the reinforcing Centaurs. Their artillery would reduce the visitor's center, which seemed to have such thick, secure walls, into rubble. With his team trapped inside.

Logan sent a silent prayer to the man upstairs even as he slapped a fresh magazine into his rifle. No matter what, he wouldn't give up, not until his last breath. Neither would his team.

But Logan grimly acknowledged that barring some kind of miracle, none of them would live to see the morning sun.

4

Spitting iron death from the repeating heavy machine guns on its chassis, the Skirmisher tracked into the visitor center. Logan flinched as its insanely powerful rounds penetrated even the thick limestone shelf he crouched upon.

Logan sent a short burst from his AX rifle at the Skirmisher, not really aiming. His purpose wasn't elimination of the target. No, Logan was perfectly okay with setting the table so Queen Bee could sit down to eat.

As the Skirmisher's tracks spun in opposite directions, causing it to pivot in place for a better shot at Logan, it exposed the two inch wide hole it its armor where its solid hydrogen fuel cell could be accessed.

Bee fired a round from her Dragoon and hit the tiny target clean. Logan squinted his eyes shut against a flash of light and heat, and the Skirmisher was no more than raining scrap.

"Great shot, Bee." Logan shouted.

"Thanks Boss, but what are we gonna do when the Centaurs and Hawks move in?" she replied.

Logan's face twisted into a defiant grimace. "Just focus on one thing at a time, Bee."

In his mind, Logan knew what they would do if the GAIN network chose to send the generation one and two heavies at his team in naked force.

They would die.

At this point, Logan had resolved himself to the fact that his mission had gone from rescue to decoy. Fire Team One would sell itself dearly to the enemy so Fire Team two could escape back to the compound. It was a sacrifice he was more than willing to make, and had sought to make many times before only to pull out victorious in the end.

Not this time, Logan thought with resignation. They'd been in tight spots before—a memory of himself crawling through a sodden storm drain to plant explosives on the coast came to his mind—but there was no way out for his team.

Maybe, though, they could distract the machines long enough for at least some of the refugees to make it to the treeline. Many would be mowed down, but if he could help it, not all.

He rose up from his crouch and ran toward the restaurant, shoving past tables and chairs stacked to form a meager defensive bulwark. Stu nearly ran into him as he led a string of terrified people, most of them women and children, out of the kitchen area.

"We're all set to go, Logan," Stu said.

Logan felt as if he'd been stabbed in the heart. He shook his head. "There's been a complication, Stu."

Stu's eyes widened with understanding as he took in Logan's grim expression. "I see. So, what's the plan?"

"We distract the enemy so my other fire team can escape," Logan said. "We—"

"What?" A man in a stained button-down shirt pushed past the line of women and children roughly to stand at their side. "Did I hear you right? You want to use us as bait so a bunch of grunts can escape? Didn't you people take an oath to protect civilian life?"

Logan's mouth twitched into a snarl, but he kept his tone civil, if a bit clipped. "Sir, I have no intention of sacrificing your life, or any of the others. You didn't let me finish. We'll try to buy you time to escape, too, and the civilians." Logan left out the part about how most of them would probably be mowed down. "But you need to listen very carefully and only run for it when I say so, y'all feel me?"

"I'm not one of your grunts, you can't order me around." The man shook his head angrily.

"Fine. Die on your own then." Logan glanced at the other civilians. "Wait for my word."

Logan and Stu ran back to the balcony at the sound of renewed gunfire. They slid to their knees, then their bellies on the limestone shelf and peered through the safety rail at the newest invader to their realm.

Three Shriekers wreaked havoc with their turret-mounted AX rifles. Their smaller ordinance couldn't penetrate the limestone balcony as the Skirmisher could, but their suppressive fire made it nigh impossible for the Shadowwalkers or Stu to take a shot.

Logan cast a glance out the busted second-story window, and gritted his teeth in frustration at the sight of the Centaurs and APCs coming in from the south, silhouetted against the night sky by the fires burning in the nearby woods.

Worse, he spied a heavy Skirmisher mounted with a dragon's breath double rifle array. The noticeable fire hazard sticker on its chassis sort of gave it away. Though it had a limited range, its incendiary ammo would set the visitor's center alight, even cracking the limestone given enough time and fuel.

Logan shouted at King. "Do you have any grenades left?"

"Negative!"

"Shit." Logan turned to Stu as bits of plaster rained down on their heads. "How about you?"

"Just one." Stu handed Logan a clearly homemade device with sloppy welds.

"What the hell is this?" Logan turned it over in his hands. "How do you even…?"

"Impact triggered. Just throw it, and don't miss."

"Suppressive fire on the Shriekers," Logan shouted. "Give me a clean toss."

"On it, Boss," Queen retorted. She and King popped out of cover and converged their fire on one of the Shriekers. Logan thought they might have disabled it, but the other machines nonetheless turned their attention away from his side of the balcony and he started running. The device in his hands felt awkward, unwieldy. And heavy. Very heavy.

Logan reached the exposed window, and the Dragon's breath Skirmisher was preparing to open fire. Its repeating Gatling cannons were spinning up. Logan heaved the blocky improvised explosive device with all his might.

It wasn't exactly the side of a barn, but neither was it an agile target wont to dodge. The square metal block hit the left rear tread of the Skirmisher, then popped in a plume of smoke and shrapnel.

The Skirmisher lifted off the ground, then did a half flip in the air before crashing on top of its chain guns. Its volatile ammunition ignited and it exploded into scrap.

Logan turned back to join the others in finishing off the Skirmishers on the lower level. As soon as the machines stopped moving, he called out to Stu. "Hey, is the rear exit clear?"

Stu rushed over to the rear second story window and peered out. "Negative. Two little treads and one big."

"We'll have to..." Logan gaped as the man who'd confronted him earlier rushed through the lower level lobby toward the rear doors. And he wasn't alone. He tugged along a young child in each hand. Logan got the feeling, looking at their terrified faces, they weren't his own. They couldn't have been older than eight or nine, a boy and a girl.

"What the hell are you doing?" Logan took aim at the man's back, though he knew he'd never get a shot off in time.

The man reached the sundered foyer and then shoved both children forward. "Run! Go, you can make it."

The boy and girl fled frantically into the open.

Logan ejected his spent magazine and slapped a fresh one—his last—into place as the man darted outside in the opposite direction the children had gone.

The children got about twelve feet before the Skirmisher and shriekers turned their weapons on them. Bullets tore the tiny children's bodies apart, leaving them only meat and blood spatter, as the man made a run for the tree line.

Logan finally got his magazine loaded, but it was too late. He shoved past Stu at the window and took aim. That asshole was not going to make it—

He fired, but only hit the side of an oak tree. Swearing, he rushed for the stairs, his face a mask of rage.

"Sergeant, stop." Stu grabbed Logan's shoulder and tried to slow him down. "It's not worth it."

"Boss, we got problems!" King pointed out the second story window toward the hairpin drive. "The Battlehawks have returned, and the new reinforcements are right behind."

Well, this is it, Logan thought to himself. *Guess no one, civilian or otherwise, is getting out of this alive after all.*

Logan joined the other Shadowwalkers at the front window. The Hawks still hadn't opened fire, though given the damage Logan and his team had inflicted to the remaining enemy units, likely that situation would change shortly. Logan wasn't sure what capabilities the strange-looking Centaurs possessed, but he was willing to bet it would be more than sufficient to kill his entire team should the Hawks fail.

To his surprise, the Centaurs fired first, lifting their arm-like appendages and unleashing powerful single shot rounds. The recoil caused their roughly humanoid "torsos" to rock back on the treaded base.

The Battlehawks each shook under the impact of the rounds a split second before they detonated in an explosion so fierce Logan could feel the heat from more than a hundred feet away. He stared in shock as the Centaurs returned to a neutral stance. The armored APC deployed the Chappie units, extending them out of its metal body on armatures. The humanoid robots dangled like fruit in the fetal position, hugging their own folded-up knees.

Row by row, they deployed and unfolded to stand at full height. Logan was perplexed when they turned their AX rifles on the returning drones, transforming Swarmers and Snappers alike into scrap metal.

"What the hell?" King turned to gape at Logan for a moment before turning his gaze back to the unlikely scene unfolding before them. "These bitches glitching or something?" He suddenly erupted in raucous laughter. "Machine bitches are glitching!"

Bee crossed herself and muttered with her eyes closed. "Thank you sweet Jesus for letting me go home to my kids."

Her prayer snapped Logan out of the discombobulated fugue the robot's internecine warfare had brought on.

"We're not out of the woods yet, Bee. We might be their next targets." Logan turned toward Purple Rain. "Sitrep?"

Purple Rain slid over to the rear window and peered out. "The bots have moved out to the front to engage the new ones. This might be our chance."

Logan nodded. "Stu, get those refugees moving! We'll maintain this position and lay down suppressive fire if need be until you're safely in the forest."

Stu grinned as he rose to his feet. "Thanks for saving my ass. Again."

Logan nodded absently. "Wish it was me." He returned to the front window. "King, they still tearing the hell out of each other?"

"Yeah, Boss. I see it, but I don't believe it." He kept his eyes on the enemy. "Maybe Bee's onto something with her white god."

"Give it a rest," Bee sneered. "At least I believe in something bigger than myself. Like you used to."

King didn't lift his gaze from the fighting robots, though his voice became heated. "If this whole clusterfuck robot apocalypse hasn't shown you there ain't no god, then I don't know what will. You saw what happened to those two kids. Why the fuck didn't *God* protect them?"

"King, I respect your right to whatever belief system you choose to—or not to—follow, but now is not the time." Logan also kept his eyes upon the two robot forces. It looked like the newer group was going to win. The heavy Centaur units were mostly staying out of it at this point, letting the Chappies handle the remaining clusters of enemies. "Whatever glitch or miracle is turning them against each other, I'm betting it won't last forever. Let's check if Stu's led the refugees clear, and make assholes and elbows ourselves."

There was no further debate after that. They descended to the first story as a drone exploded right outside the front foyer. Bits of broken glass and rubble rained down from the ceiling as a Chappie marched past, its gun aimed at the sky in an attempt to annihilate more drones. The robot seemed oblivious to Logan and the others hunkered inside the building. If he wanted to, he could have engaged and shot it down. That didn't seem wise at the moment, considering it would only alert the other new robots to his presence. And probably piss them off.

Logan peered past the Chappie to the larger battlefield. Drones buzzed about and exploded crazily in the sky, sometimes taking some of the Chappies with them. Meanwhile, the burning wrecks of the Battlehawks stood in a grim line before the larger Centaurs, who just remained still as statues—they were likely unable to accurately target the faster moving drones.

If the Battlehawks had been tough, the upgraded Centaurs would be sheer brutality. How could humanity hope to defeat an ever-evolving robot army? Without that glitch, they'd be goners right now.

Logan joined King, Purple Rain, and Bee at the foyer exit. "Did Stu get them clear?"

"They're clear Boss." King jutted his chin toward the tree line. "Should we hotfoot it?"

"Yeah, but not assholes and elbows," Logan said. "Tactical retrograde."

"I'm moving out." Purple Rain rushed for a shorn-off tree trunk thirty yards from the rear exit and threw himself down behind it. A moment later his shoulders and head reappeared as he aimed his AX rifle around the bole of the trunk.

"You're up next, Bee," Logan said.

"Copy that, Boss." Queen slung her rifle over her shoulder and rushed out toward a rocky outcropping. Once she was ensconced behind it, barrel pointed toward the melee evolving in the hairpin drive, King went next, followed by Rocko.

His target was a thick oak tree trunk about twenty yards beyond Bee. Logan started moving as soon as Rocko was in position, angling his trajectory to take him behind the crumbling, low foundation of a long-gone building.

In such a manner, they covered their retreat.

Logan made it to the tree line and rejoined the rest of his team. Stu was there as well, along with what was left of the refugees. He made eye contact with Stu, his smile fading. "Did you see where that son of a bitch went?"

Stu knew exactly to whom Logan was referring. "No. Never liked that guy, but didn't think he'd use orphaned kids as cannon fodder to save his own sorry ass. If I had, I'd have put a round in him a long time ago."

Logan clapped him on the shoulder. "You never know someone's character until they get put under pressure. I mean, deep, real, battlefield pressure. I'm glad you stepped up when so many others stepped back."

Stu clasped the hand on his shoulder. "Likewise."

Logan went over to Rocko, who peered through his goggles in telescopic mode. "How's the battle going?"

"Looks like it's mostly over." Rocko shook his head. "Never seen a malfunction like this. The GAIN system attacking its own army?"

"Maybe there's a hacker?" Logan suggested. "A human who's managed to gain access to one of the decentralized server farms?"

Rocko lifted the goggles for a moment to gaze right into Logan's eyes. "Maybe, but it would take an intellect better than Albert Einstein and Stephen Hawking combined to figure it out. I was thinking something not so comforting."

Logan sighed. "Damn it all, Rocko, can you go five minutes without pissing me off?"

Rocko's eyes widened, and Logan sighed.

"No, no, come on." Logan made a motion with his hand. "Come on, out with it. Sorry to bite your head off, but you've got to admit you're a pain in the ass most of the time."

"Ah, okay, Boss." Rocko swallowed. "I was thinking, maybe one of the cloned, decentralized systems decided it wants to be the only show in town."

Logan shook his head. "Speculation is pointless. What happened, happened. Take another gander and tell me if you think they're fixing to come after us now."

Rocko pulled the goggles back down and frowned. "The second wave seems to have won, but taken heavy casualties. They're loading up the APC with what's left of their Chappies, and the Centaurs have already left."

"Bitches aren't even trying to look for us?" King asked.

"Nope," Rocko said.

"I'd love to know where our erstwhile cavalry is heading," Logan said.

In that moment, Chief and Cowboy returned, joining Logan and the others beneath the trees.

"I thought I told you to flee," Logan said.

Chief shrugged. "We did flee. Got pinned. But then the cavalry came." He nodded toward the retreating machines.

Logan felt a sudden dread in the pit of his stomach. "Doc and Twigg?"

"Doc is bringing Twigg to the ATVs," Chief said. "Man, Twigg…"

"Is he okay?" Logan pursed his lips in concern.

"Okay?" Chief replied. "You should have seen him. He turned around and solo killed a drone and two Skirmishers with one long burst."

"Holy hippo spit." Logan laughed. "Guess we can't call him green anymore."

"Nope, Cowboy already designated him Cutter."

"Fitting name, ain't it!" Cowboy said with a wide grin.

Chief's gaze returned to the horizon, and the machines silhouetted by the fires that yet burned in the night. "Let me track them. Find their base."

"Too dangerous," Logan said. "Just because those

bots attacked their own doesn't mean they're on our side."

"It doesn't mean they are *not* on our side, either." Chief grinned. "I'll be careful. The spirits will protect me."

"I'm going with you," Cowboy said.

The Chief looked to Logan for confirmation, who nodded. Two was better than one, and the big southerner could meld into the wilderness better than most.

As they headed into the forest in pursuit, he prayed for their safe return, even as he puzzled over the mystery of this most recent turn in events.

5

The golden dawn of the new day kissed the landscape with its cheerful light, but did little to lift Logan's spirits, nor those of the refugee band the Shadowwalkers had rescued from the rest area.

"Hey, Boss?" Stu approached Logan quietly, his tone careful and low. Logan didn't remark on his call sign being Stu's new default. "Are we going to get moving soon? The younger kids are getting restless."

Logan sighed, and rubbed a hand down his tired face. Children in the theater of war had been an occupational hazard since before the Advent of the machines. He felt drained, but kept it out of his tone and banned it from his decisions.

"We need to hang tight for a spell, Stu. The machines, they're expecting us to run for our hideaway." Logan put his arm on the man's shoulder and pointed, guiding his vision. "You see those little specks in the distance?"

Stu gazed toward the horizon. "I see them. Drones."

"Probably Snappers," Logan agreed, "maybe even some explosive Swarmers, too. They've been moving in a standard sweep pattern, beating the bush as it were, looking for us. But more importantly, watching which way we run. We need to wait it out a bit, and let the heat die down. Plus, the satellites will be passing by soon. We have to hunker down."

Stu nodded, and Logan could tell he didn't want to argue the point. But he pressed on anyway. "So, ah, how long will that be?"

"How long?" Logan shrugged. "Don't rightly know. The AI is keen on efficiency. If its search proves fruitless for a couple hours, it'll probably reign in those expensive little drones. Suckers eat up their batteries right quick, and they're not easy or efficient to recharge."

"All right, fair enough. I'll try and get the refugees settled down."

"I'd appreciate it greatly, Stu." Logan grabbed Stu's arm before he could turn to leave. "Oh, and Stu? Sweep's starting soon. Make sure nobody leaves cover."

Stu nodded, squeezed Logan's arm back, and returned to his charges. Logan didn't envy the man, but he did admire him.

Of course, Stu had just accepted his authority, so really any burdens placed on Stu were by proxy placed upon him. Logan liked being a Staff Sergeant, or at least he had. He preferred leading his small but elite unit to the crass bureaucracy of higher command.

Logan bowed his head to pass under a low hanging branch as he entered a dense copse of deciduous trees. Within their sheltering boughs, the rest of his team was taking a much-needed rest. Unfortunately, two of them were going to go back to work early.

"Purple Rain, Cutter," Logan said.

Purple Rain lifted his head from the pack he'd been using as a pillow and squirmed to his feet. The newly named Cutter wasn't asleep, but was telling some of the younger refugees about his heroics on the field of battle earlier.

Logan was glad Cutter had gotten a win during the conflict, so long as Cutter's confidence didn't turn into careless arrogance.

They assembled in front of Logan, and he crossed his arms over his chest as he looked them both over. "We're going to have to lie low for a couple hours till the heat dies down, and then another couple hours most likely until the latest satellite sweep is over."

They nodded, almost in unison. Purple Rain stretched his neck to get the kinks out, already preparing for what was to come next.

"I need the two of you to act as our spotters," Logan said. "Let me know if a bot or a drone comes near our position."

Purple Rain nodded, then turned to Cutter. "I'll take the northeast quadrant, you take southwest?"

Cutter sighed. "Fine."

They trudged off to do their duty. Logan had full confidence they would not waver, and regretted having to cut their rest short. But they were the company's point men, and the youngest members at that.

Logan sat on one of the shrouded ATVs and mopped the sweat off his brow. In the deep woods like this, the wind had trouble freshening the air. He took a long pull from his canteen before screwing the lid on tight and leaning back on his cushioned, camo sheeted perch.

"You look worried, Boss."

He started as Ripley sat next to him. She bit off the end of a piece of beef jerky and handed it to him. Logan took it with a smile and popped it in his mouth. "Mmm. That's right delightful. Where'd you come across this culinary confection?"

"I love it when you talk all southern." Ripley chuckled. "One of the refugees had some. Made it himself from boar. We should herd pigs, Logan. I miss bacon."

Logan put his finger to his lips and glanced around. No one seemed to be paying them the slightest attention. Ripley rolled her eyes.

"Okay, 'Boss,' I forgot. Can't let on to the team about our extracurricular stress relief activities." Ripley sighed. "So, are you going to tell me what's on your mind?"

He gazed at her crossly. "What's on my mind is how hard it is to keep pigs. It takes a lot of water, Rip, and it's a powerful stench—"

"Not that, you cornpone twit." Ripley smacked him on the arm playfully. "What's got you so eaten up?"

"I'm worried about Chief and Cowboy," Logan said.

She nodded. "They'll be okay. They're big boys."

Logan smiled fleetingly. "Yeah."

Her brows drew together. "I wonder if the bots really are turning on each other. Maybe there's a rogue faction of good robots?" She looked at Logan for a long moment, then shrugged. "Feel like committing some fraternization? Help get your mind off certain... problems. Besides, I could use a good dressing down. Maybe some discipline?"

She slid off the ATV and sauntered off, swinging her hips far more than was necessary. Logan sighed, but he did feel a little bit better.

He prayed to the man upstairs that he watch over Chief and Cowboy, even though the Indian was technically a heathen. Logan figured God knew who was good and who was bad no matter what kind of church they went to, or none at all.

Hopefully this would be one of those times the man upstairs was all New Testament and forgiveness, and not Old Testament fire and brimstone.

Lying stock still in the tall, wavering grass, Chief peered intently across the two-lane service road which meandered away from the highway to give access to a somewhat rustic but nonetheless busy truck stop.

Or at least, it had been busy before GAIN took over piloting the goods and services vehicles instead of humans. Now it was a rusted old relic, barely able to stay in business before the Advent because of a small trailer park community nearby who utilized it as a convenience store.

It had taken the machines longer to reach it than the major population centers. While he and Cowboy had been tracking the rogue machines, they'd come across the trailer park in question. Much like the homes they'd come across in the south, the doors had been torn asunder and there were no living humans present.

The Centaurs had continued on past the exit leading to the trailer park, but some of the Skirmishers and Shriekers had veered off, apparently to investigate. But if the machines had already killed off the trailer park's denizens, why did they need to return?

To their surprise, the tracked cobots had deployed solar panels from the top of their chassis and remained in the trailer park for an entire afternoon to recharge. That was an upgrade which didn't bode well for their resistance band. Solar panels would greatly expand their range of influence, since they no longer had to return to a charging station.

He and Cowboy, deciding the bots weren't going anywhere until sunset, retreated back to where they'd stashed their muffled ATVs and rested, alternating who was on watch so one of them was always awake. The spy satellites were out that night, so they had to be careful to remain beneath the cover of the nearby forest. Chief managed to pin a timber rattler to the ground with a well-timed knife throw, providing sustenance beyond their field rations.

When less than an hour remained until sunset, they'd mounted the ATVs and, staying beneath the canopy of the forest for cover, they traveled to a ridge where they could overlook the trailer park. The tracked machines tore out just after sunset and rejoined the main highway. Since there was currently a hole in the satellite sweeps, Chief and Cowboy followed the roundabout way, until they reached the truck stop grocery store, where several of the bots had stopped.

"Chief, what you think is going on here?" Cowboy asked.

Chief glanced at Cowboy and grunted noncommittally before answering. "My best guess? Mexican standoff."

Cowboy frowned. "How you figure?"

"See the bots on the south end of the parking lot?" Chief pointed that way.

"Yeah, I see 'em," Cowboy said. "Whole lot of generation one trackers, couple squadrons of drones."

"I believe they're in opposition to the bots we've been following," Chief said. "See how they've formed up a defensive line, with the tracked cobots in front of the APCs, which in turn provide cover for the Centaurs?"

Cowboy clucked his tongue and shook his bald head. "I reckon you're right. That makes it the second time these rogues we've been following have fought against other robots. What gives?"

"I don't know," Chief said.

"What do you want to do?" Cowboy asked.

"For now, keep watch and wait," Chief replied.

Cowboy sighed. "I was afraid you'd say that. Why don't they attack?"

"For the generation one side, I believe they realize that though they have the opposition vastly outnumbered, they are lacking in firepower," Chief explained. "Namely, they have no answer to the Centaurs. As for the other side... I'm not sure. But I have a hunch. Stay here while I test something."

Chief low-crawled away several feet, then stood up, exposing himself.

"What are you doing?" Cowboy hissed from where he remained lying down.

Chief made sure to keep out of visual range of the generation one swarm, but he was in full view of one of the deployed Chappies. It pointedly turned its head his way, then pivoted back toward the opposing bots, ignoring Chief entirely. It had flagged him as a non-threat.

Chief dropped, and crawled back to Cowboy.

"Are you crazy, Chief?" Cowboy said. "You trying to get us killed? You know how mad my wife would be if I get killed out here?"

"Calm yourself." Chief pointed at the newer robot force. "If they wanted us dead, they would already have killed us. I suspect that they've known we followed them the entire way since the rest stop."

"So what are you saying?" Cowboy said. "That they consider us hardly worthy of their attention? That we're little more than flies to them, not worth even attacking?"

"It's a change from how the other robots behave, is it not?" Chief said. "I needed to prove that they won't attack humans upon sight, like the other machines. If they were a decentralized clone engaged in a power struggle with the main AI, I'm certain their programming would have impelled them to fire on me. They did not. I think there's a good possibility they're on our side. Whether they've been hacked, or what, doesn't matter. We need to trust the spirits and not question this gift." Motion drew his gaze past the covering foliage. "They're on the move. We should retreat a safe distance."

They made their way back to a slight rise in the terrain and hunkered down behind a fallen tree trunk. Chief peered over the moss-encrusted surface as the tracked vehicles surged forward. He couldn't see all of the battle, but it seemed as if some of the bots were being used to draw off the bomber drones from the gen one side.

A veteran soldier and fire team leader, he could see the strategy in play before the gen one robots did.

The "good" robot force prodded them into taking the offensive; one of the Centaurs had doubled back to come at them from the rear, and flushed them out of the tree line. The remaining Centaurs opened fire with their anti-tank rounds.

Chief plugged his ears, and Cowboy did a moment later. The detonations were so intense they shook the trees and blew a nimbus of dust over their position.

"Sheeit." Cowboy whistled through his teeth. "Who do you figure won?"

"Who do you think?" Chief rose from his crouch and hustled back to the service road. When he reached it, the generation one army lay in ruins, as well as some of the "good" force. The good robots were withdrawing, but one of them had remained behind, a Skirmisher with a black and gold paint job. Chief and Cowboy took cover behind an abandoned Texas barrier.

"What's it doing?" Cowboy unslung his assault rifle.

Chief laid a hand on the barrel before he could aim it. "Be still, and knowledge will reveal itself to you."

"Old reservation proverb?"

"Read it in a fortune cookie," Chief replied. "It's using that manipulator arm to draw something in the dirt."

In moments the black and gold Skirmisher finished its task, and pivoted on alternating tracks to face them. Chief and Cowboy ducked.

A moment later, the crunch of gravel beneath treads grew softer in volume. Chief peered past his cover in time to watch the Skirmisher trundle off, increasing speed to catch up with its fellows.

When it was gone, Chief and Cowboy warily approached the spot where it had written something in the dirt.

"Them are coordinates," Cowboy announced.

"It would appear so," Chief agreed. "I believe it's time to return to Logan and inform him of our findings."

"By the way, did you notice that the machines left the trailer park only after the spy satellites had passed out of range?" Cowboy said. "Just as if they're avoiding the satellite sweeps. Like us Shadowwalkers."

"I noticed this, yes," Chief said.

Cowboy glanced toward the truck stop. "Should we check to see if any refugees are holed up in the park grocery?"

Chief considered for a moment, then nodded. "We check, then head home."

LOGAN GREW INCREASINGLY anxious as the days passed and Cowboy and Chief failed to return, though he tried to hide it well.

Ever since he had returned to the compound with the others, Mara, Cowboy's wife, had taken to glaring at him at every opportunity. She didn't like having her husband going out on sorties. As far as she was concerned, Cowboy's contributions to the effort were his compound, which he had built with her trust fund.

Logan wasn't sure how much longer they could stay there. The machines probably suspected there was a human compound in the vicinity by now. He had doubled the watch, and revamped the existing evacuation plan. He also had the soldiers and civilians run through tactical retrograde drills twice a day—if enemy units were sighted, he needed everyone to retreat to one of the planned fallback points as quickly as possible. He remembered how efficiently the robots had destroyed Fort Benning, and he knew if an attack came, the refugees would have precious few moments to retreat.

Logan tried to busy his mind with thoughts of other matters. Ron Ditgen had harvested a record yield from his mushroom farm. Logan hadn't been a huge fan of eating fungus before, but some of the mushrooms Ditgen's crew could grow tasted great, even like meat.

They were high in vitamin D as well, which was important since due to the satellite sweeps and drones almost nobody got enough sunlight to generate their own. Doc kept a careful watch on camp nutrition, and he highly approved of the mushroom rich diet.

When he had a rare idle moment to himself, Logan pondered what their next move should be. They'd tried direct action before, and destroyed the GAIN network's Washington DC nexus. That was supposed to have been it, the end. But their AI adversary had decentralized itself to protect against such an easy termination. At least that was the theory.

They'd returned to the compound, ostensibly to regroup but Logan and pretty much everyone else had concluded the fight wouldn't be won in their lifetime. It was time to figure out how to survive during the machine occupation and work on enacting some form of resistance later, after they'd gotten better footing.

And truth be told, before the battle at the rest stop a few days back, he'd have never considered resistance a real possibility. But if somehow, some way, a portion of the bot army had gone rogue, then it turned the odds from none to slim. And it meant that there was a possibility more of the robots could be turned.

But still, before he decided on what to do, he needed to wait until Cowboy and Chief returned. He was starting to wonder just how far away this robot base must be. And he was also considering the possibility that his friends had been slaughtered by the very same machines they had been sent to track.

The morning of the fourth day came, and when still the pair hadn't returned, he considered sending a sortie to search for them.

"Something eating you, Boss?" Ripley buttoned up her shirt, legs kicked under his bunk.

"No," he said. "Just worried about Chief and Cowboy. Why, something eating you?"

She chuckled. "Not anymore."

Ripley rose to her feet and smiled on her way out of the tent. Logan grinned ear to ear for a moment, glad to have such a pleasant distraction, but his thoughts quickly returned to more somber matters.

He checked his goggles. Good, no satellite sweep for another hour. Plenty of time to round up a sortie. Who to send? Himself and Purple Rain, for sure. Probably need Doc just in case—

The sound of a forest owl hooting three times reached his ears. The scouts…

Logan stood up and excitedly hooted back.

He met Chief at the perimeter of camp, Cowboy coming in a few seconds later. They handed off their weapons to Mara, who pecked Cowboy on the lips before calling on King's kid to get the men some water from the purifier.

"Glad you made it back, old friend." Logan clasped Chief's hand. "You too, Cowboy."

"Thanks Boss." Cowboy turned toward Chief. "You want to tell him or should I?"

Chief accepted a cup full of water and drained it in one go. "We tracked the rogue bots for a couple days up the interstate. Twice we watched them liberate humans besieged by generation one bots."

"Fuck all that, Chief, can't you tell a damn story?" Cowboy said. "That's boring as hell. Tell him about Goldie."

Chief shot Cowboy a look of patiently restrained frustration, before turning back to Logan. "The Goldie he refers to is a Skirmisher with a black and gold color scheme. And Dragon's Breath cannons."

"Nasty," Logan said. "What happened?"

"It wrote something in the dirt after the second conflict," Chief replied. "Coordinates. 37.5597° N, 88.6617° W."

"Somewhere around abouts the Illinois/Kentucky border, by our figuring," Cowboy explained.

Logan frowned, and scratched his chin. "There's a national forest around that area. Shawnee Forest. My pop took me fishing there once. Best damn bluegill I ever tasted."

Ditgen shouldered his way past the Shadowwalkers who had gathered to greet the returning soldiers.

Logan turned his way and arched an eyebrow. "Can I help you, Mr. Ditgen?"

"Actually, I may be able to help you." Ditgen gestured toward Chief and Cowboy. "Those coordinates you mentioned, near Shawnee National Forest? I'm pretty certain they would be right on top of a major branch of the Cave-In-Rock cavern system."

"The what, now?" Logan asked.

"It's one of the larger cavern systems in Illinois." Ditgen grinned. "Underground engineer, remember? This stuff is a hobby. If someone has figured out how to reprogram the bots, then they could do worse for a hideaway than a cavern system."

"They'd sure be safe from satellites, sweeps or no." Logan nodded.

Bee stepped forward. "We got to go check it out. I mean, if there's someone else fighting the good fight, and they've got their own bot army—"

"Then they might be able to teach us how to get our own," Logan finished. "All right, Shadowwalkers. Get some rest, because we're road tripping tomorrow at oh nine hundred."

Logan felt a tinge of something he hadn't felt in a long time. It was nearly midnight before he realized it was hope.

6

A chill drop in temperatures overnight birthed the thick fog that clung to the forest floor early on the morning Logan and the Shadowwalkers planned to leave the compound.

Queen Bee hugged her husband and children close, wearing her full gear but still managing to look motherly.

Purple Rain stood near Logan, a thoughtful light in his eyes. "You ever regret not getting married, Boss?"

Logan shook his head curtly. "Nope. Not one bit. Especially the way the world's gone to shit since the GAIN AI attained sentience. Obviously, the man upstairs fingered me for something different."

"Yeah, but…don't you regret not being able to leave behind a legacy?" Rain shifted a bit and laid his heavy pack on the ground as he adjusted the straps. "I mean, spread the seed, as it were?"

Logan smiled gently, and gestured toward Bee and her family. "Way I see it, I have a lot of kids. The children I liberated from a human trafficking ring in

Borneo are my kids. The children born to hostages I rescued are my kids. Hell, Purple Rain, in a lot of ways, you're one of my kids. And I'm a proud poppa, you feel me?"

"Oh." Purple Rain looked away and blinked rapidly. "I—see. Boss, I've always looked up to…"

"Save it. I've done about all the emoting I can for one day." They both burst into laughter as King, walking rapidly on stiff legs, strode up. He dropped his pack in front of them and pointed back the way he'd come.

"Boss, you can't let him bring that abomination," King said. He squeezed his wife and children in a great bear hug before she shooed them along.

"Might help if I had some context, King," Logan said. "Let who bring what abomination in particular?"

As if on cue, the strains of "In a Godda Da Vida" reached their ears, played on an accordion—poorly. Rocko strode up, wearing his full gear but also sporting his treasured if somewhat trail worn accordion.

"Rocko." Logan sighed. "Rocko!"

Rocko ceased what he no doubt thought of as masterful playing, his eyes widening in query. "Yeah, Boss?"

"No, son." Logan shook his head. "Just no."

Rocko's shoulders slumped, and he shuffled back toward the compound entrance to stow the accordion.

King shot Logan a grateful look. "Thanks, Boss."

"It was for everyone's benefit, King." Logan frowned as Ripley and Double A strode up, wearing their full gear. "This ain't an air force gig, y'all. It's going to be hard travelling and an uncertain future."

Ripley arched an eyebrow. "And that's different from the usual how?"

Double A chuckled. "This time it'll be easier. She doesn't have a broken leg to rehab and I don't have a shark bite killing me."

"Come on, Boss." Ripley grinned. "You know you could use an extra pair of hands."

Logan felt a bit of flush come to his cheeks.

Double A added his two cents. "We're trained fighters too, Boss. Besides, I'm a pararescueman and you never know when you might need Rip's skillset, like with the ECMs last time."

Logan stroked his chin and nodded. "All right, then. If y'all so eager to get shot at by soulless robots, then who am I to argue?" He chuckled as Cowboy practically ran from his wife Mara as she hollered instructions at him.

Cowboy dashed up to their gathering huddle and gazed hopefully at Logan. "Boss, please say it's time to deploy."

Logan smiled patiently. "Still waiting on Doc and Cutter. And Chief is gassing up the ATVs and checking oil and tire pressure." He glanced at the ammo shed, and had a thought. "Be right back."

Logan went to the shed and entered. The team had taken roughly half the ammunition allocated to the compound. He knelt, and pulled out a box of magazines in one corner, and dug through them until he spotted one marked with yellow tape.

Cowboy's wife had worked for Smith and Wesson, and had experimented with explosive rounds for their AX rifles. However, they were dangerous. About one shot out of two jammed in the barrel, and about half of those exploded. She had abandoned the project, and this was the last explosive magazine still in existence.

Logan stared at it for a long moment. A round like this could make all the difference in a pinch. Assuming it worked.

If I use this, I could die.

He gingerly scooped the yellow-taped magazine out of the box and shoved it into his pack.

"What was that all about?" Chief asked when he returned.

"Just doing one last quick ammo count," Logan lied.

Once the team was fully assembled, Logan shook hands with Stu Redding. He also spoke to Hanky Bob and Redding about camp safety while the Shadowwalkers were gone. "Remember, at the first sign of trouble, relocate the civilians to the safest fallback point. Keep practicing the evacuation drills with everyone twice a day."

"Understood," Hanky Bob said. "We won't let you down."

Logan nodded, then he and the others headed down to the ravine where they stored their ATV fleet beneath camo sheets.

Logan checked the status of the satellite sweep and found that it had ended just minutes ago. "Can't ask for a more auspicious start. Okay, Shadowwalkers, we're playing this one by the book. Use the trails we've blazed already as much as possible, avoid the main roads, and always keep an eye out for drones." Logan turned toward Cutter. "Your new callsign is prophetic, Twigg, since you're in charge of cutting through any fences we come across."

The company laughed as King placed the wire cutters lovingly in Cutter's grip.

"Not all heroes wear capes." King patted him firmly on the back.

"Ha ha, asshole." Cutter secured the clippers onto his vehicle as Logan and Mason plotted their route using the augmented reality goggles. The terrain mapping feature meant the team could set virtual waypoints that only appeared on the goggles. This allowed the team to travel at a larger distance from each other and increased their chances of moving stealthily. The only drawback was that since they preferred to keep the goggles in read only mode, they had to manually input the waypoints into each pair.

As usual, fire team two went first, while Logan's team brought up the rear with him coming dead last. Using his goggles, he could not only see the virtual waypoints and directions on where to turn, but track his allies as well. Their line was spread out over a mile, minimizing risk of detection.

In a way, Logan was glad to be back on the trail again. The pressures of running the camp were now literally miles behind him. Out here with his team, rolling and rocking along on a vehicle he'd learned to handle expertly, was as close to a vacation as he could hope for.

Logan realized he was kidding himself. He'd never been the type of man to take a vacation. If he wasn't doing something after a couple of days in a row, he'd go stir crazy and lose his mind.

They sheltered in an old gray barn in a field overgrown by weeds, far from the highway, as the next satellite sweep neared. Doc freaked out a bit because of a few hornet nests inside the barn. Apparently, he was allergic. Cowboy's solution was to draw his sidearm and shoot the nests down, but Logan put the kibbash on any insecticide.

"You leave them alone, they'll leave you alone," Logan said. "You shoot those nests, you'll just make things worse. Doc. Just relax."

They drank from their canteens, enjoyed a small snack of dried catfish jerky, which everyone but Rocko was a fan of–he claimed it gave him heartburn.

Eating a peaceful lunch in a cool, shaded barn in the middle of an open field? Sure didn't seem like any apocalypse Logan had ever seen. Then he admonished himself. The shooting, screaming, blood and death could resume at any moment. No point in tempting fate.

Once the satellite sweep ended, the Shadowwalkers were on the move again. But Cutter, their pointman, wound up calling for a halt barely an hour into their next window. The news was spread down the line by hand signals.

By the time Logan and the others joined up with the rest of the crew, Cutter was returning from the edge of the forest with Cowboy, where the pair had ostensibly ventured to scout.

Logan parked his ATV along with the others under the shade of trees clinging to a hillside, then dismounted. "What's the good word? Why'd you call a halt?"

Cutter's face was pale, and a sheen of sweat only partly brought on by the day's heat shone on his forehead.

"Crossing the highway might be a lot harder than we thought." Cutter offered his goggles to Logan, who donned them. On the display was a map with several red X's marked upon it.

"What am I looking at?" Logan asked.

"The bots have set up garrisons or roadblocks at

these points," Cutter replied.

Logan sighed. "All the good places to cross with our ATVs. Cowboy was right. They know we've got a stronghold somewhere in this area."

"Told you, Boss." Cowboy sighed. "But it is what it is. How are we going to play this?"

"Should we send someone back to warn our families?" Bee asked, the concern for her children obvious in her voice.

Logan shook his head. "Negative. We already suspected as much, and doubled the watch, if you recall. Stu and the others are still practicing the evac drills twice a day. If the enemy finds our compound, the soldiers will get everyone out."

At least, that was what he hoped.

"We could move our families now..." King suggested.

"No," Logan said. "They're safer in the compound, for the time being. The robots have to search a huge swath of land. Their chances of finding the compound are extremely small. Needle in a haystack small. We continue on our mission. When we return, we'll discuss relocation."

Logan focused on the virtual world on the goggles. "This garrison has only twenty bots, according to Cutter's report. That's the weak spot."

"Ah, Boss, I should tell you that particular garrison is small for a reason," Cutter said. "One of that twenty is a Reaper tripod."

Bee kicked a pine cone to shatter into oblivion against a tree trunk. "A Reaper? That should have been the first thing you mentioned. The *first* thing."

"I took out one before..." Purple Rain said calmly.

"Yeah, when you had buildings for cover," Bee said. "We got none of that here."

"We don't need to take it out." Logan removed the goggles and offered them to Bee. "The Reaper only moves about six miles per hour. See the overpass a mile down the road? We make our crossing there. We may still have to engage the faster bots, the Skirmishers and Shriekers, but that big boy and the Chappies will take longer to reach the theater of battle. We bound across, laying down suppressive fire, and don't worry about taking down big boy."

"Do we have to fight them at all?" Ripley said. "Maybe we can sneak across at night."

Cutter shook his head. "They all have nightvision. Not only that, but there's a heavy Snapper presence all along the main roads. We're going to be spotted within seconds of the crossing."

Logan slid his own goggles back on and considered the map once more. "There are other places to cross."

"What about the concrete dividers separating the lanes in these 'other' places?" Purple Rain asked. "We can't bring our ATVs over them. Unless you mean backtracking for days…"

"We'll find a way without backtracking too far." Logan glanced at Cowboy, who raised his eyebrows in anticipation. "But we'll have to move quickly either way." He pursed his lips and considered each member of the squad. "Once the GAIN network knows we're on the move in the area, it could decide to send in heavy air support units. Things we don't stand a chance against unless we get some cover. But I know this team, and I know we can do this. Is everybody on the same page, here?"

The Shadowwalkers were tense, but they also seemed satisfied with Logan's plan.

All except for Rocko. "Boss, I hate to be a party pooper—"

"When has that ever stopped you before?" King and Bee high-fived as the rest of the company save Logan and Chief laughed.

"Go on, Rocko." Logan prompted.

"Right. Are the vague promises of a 'good' robot army worth risking our lives for?" Rocko asked. "I know I'm the new guy here, but if the bots are onto us having a stronghold in this area, we need to fucking move that stronghold. That should be our priority, not trying to hook up with R2D2 and Threepio because an erector set wrote some numbers in the dirt. Sure, you got an evac plan in place, but will it be enough?"

King inhaled deeply through his nostrils, and then let it out in a long sigh. "Man's got a point, Boss. Not that it isn't important to maybe find out what's what with these 'good' robots, but there's going to be a shit ton of heat on us the whole way north. Maybe moving the stronghold should be the priority?"

Logan glanced from King to Rocko and chuckled. "Never thought I'd see the day the two of you are in agreement. Look, y'all, I considered staying home and hunkering down, or trying to move or expand our stronghold, but consider this: by moving north, there's a good chance we'll draw these machines *away* from the compound, potentially negating the need for us to move it. Besides, as I explained to y'all before, the rogue AI is dedicated to its mission of reducing the human population to a tiny, manageable number. It wants us to be animals in a zoo, preserved but not free. If there's a chance, even a small one, that we can find a way to use the machines against each other, we need to take it. Also, consider this: how do we know those blockades are for us? Maybe the machines are trying to catch these 'good' bots."

He turned his gaze upon each of his squad in turn. Cowboy nodded, but he was always up for action. Chief remained as stalwart as ever. If Logan told Chief to jump off a cliff for the good of the mission, Chief would suggest a backward somersault thrown in on the way down.

King and Bee seemed conflicted. Both had family back at the compound, but neither voiced further complaints. Cutter's mother and father dwelled at the compound as well, but their wellbeing didn't weight as heavily on his young mind as Bee's family did on hers.

Ripley seemed determined to do her part no matter what, which Logan knew was her way of making sure everyone understood she intended to pull her weight. Logan was fairly certain everyone knew about them sharing a cot now and again, though no one had been crass enough to mention it to his face.

Doc had adopted a kind of "to hell with it" grin, something Logan didn't like much. Hopeless soldiers put themselves and everyone around them at risk, and Logan intended to go on living—so long as it didn't conflict with his self-imposed mission of saving humanity.

"We can't just sit around and wait," Logan said. "This enemy isn't going to be overthrown by a revolution, or mellow out with a new generation, or be assassinated by its underlings. It's relentless, indefatigable. Worse, it's not remaining stagnant. It's growing, evolving, building more and better machines to kill us even more efficiently." Logan chuckled helplessly. "I'd love to just hang out in a cave eating blueberry pie and sipping sweet tea for the rest of my life. Believe me, if we could win this war by doing that, I'd be all over that shit."

The squad rippled with soft, nervous laughter.

"If we keep going," Logan continued. "We're going to have to fight, maybe even to the death. But it's the same if we turn back. It's a scenario we've been in often enough before. Battle is in our future pretty much no matter what. But we're Rangers. Battle is part of who we are. We fight them, as much as possible, on our terms. We're not jarheads. We don't go in guns blazing thinking we're goddamn invincible. We go in careful, we go in with strategy, and we get out of those sticky situations with the lowest mother fucking casualty count of any squad in Ranger history. Why?"

The question hung in the air for a moment before Cowboy leaped to his feet. "Cause we're the Shadow-mother-fucking-walkers."

Logan grinned as the rest of the squad took up the shout. But he had to toss cold water on their enthusiasm. "Great, y'all. Now shut up before you bring a drone army down on our asses."

7

Logan moved twenty feet behind Bee as fire team one bounded past team two's covered position a stone's throw from the silent gray highway. So far, the only movement anyone had detected had come from wildlife. An eight-point buck had bounded away from Logan, and for a moment he worried that it had given away their position. But the machines did not open fire.

A half-moon cast silver light over the eight-lane highway, its edges overgrown with weeds and overhang from the trees. It didn't look that extensive on paper, but to Logan's eyes it seemed a wide expanse where they would be hopelessly exposed to the enemy. The night vision mode of his goggles cast everything in a pall of green.

The sturdy concrete dividers which split the north and southbound lanes in two posed another problem for their crossing, as Purple Rain had previously mentioned. Ripley, whose father worked in construction, assured them that each six-foot section weighed more than a ton. Moving them was not an option.

Fortunately, his crew were nothing if not resourceful. Cowboy had been an avid outdoorsman before the Advent, and one of his favorite things to do was get drunk, then build ramps and jump his ATV over the dividers with likeminded Rangers.

Thus, he had the knowledge necessary to calculate a risky but undeniably swift way to get their ATVs over the barrier: a ramp.

A greasy spoon restaurant they'd sheltered in the night before gave them that ramp. They had retreated to said restaurant, and Purple Rain had shimmied up to the top of a twenty-foot post, getting red rust all over his fatigues. He cut the bolts clean off, allowing the twelve-foot long, five-foot-wide sign to drop to the ground.

It was thick steel alloy, ideally suited for their purpose. Fortunately, their ramp only had to be one way. Getting it into position required a tow from an ATV, then Chief and Rocko would set up the ramp, leaning it against the concrete barrier.

It was a lot of work just to get their vehicles over, but this was the least protected crossing for at least twenty miles. And it was a long walk to the Kentucky/Illinois border. The ATVs would cut days off their journey.

The vehicles were a vital resource that had to be accounted for and preserved. Logan began to regret shooting down Chief's suggestion that they utilize horses rather than ATVs. Even a plow horse could have jumped that barrier. Then again, there had been the small problem of finding suitable riding horses...

Purple Rain cut through the fence sundering the tree line from the interstate and moved swiftly across the dark highway. He flattened himself against the thick concrete pillars supporting the overpass and then unshouldered his rifle. Rain crouched behind the pillar and kept watch at the garrison of bots at the much larger and easier to access overpass a mile up the road. There were more bots manning a roadblock a similar distance away in the opposite direction, but they were currently concealed by a rise in the road.

King went next, choosing a different pillar. Then Bee, who crouched behind an overturned flatbed truck which had been charred by a fire. Logan grimly noted the blackened skeleton, barely visible in the moonlight, still in the driver's seat.

Now it was his turn. He moved past Bee and crouched near the end of the flatbed trailer. He peered out at the distant enemy, and then at the sky. No drones. Maybe the squad could get out of this without having to fight after all—

Logan froze. He quickly signaled Chief. Hold position.

Beneath the overpass, he saw hundreds of Snapper and Swarmer drones. They were plugged into a structure built into the underside of the bridge: a charging station.

If any of those drones finished its charging cycle and deployed, it would spot them immediately. And probably activate all the others.

That, or another drone could happen along at any time to plug itself into the charging network. Same results. They could never hope to outrun or outfight so many drones at once, even if they didn't have to deal with the garrisons further up and down the highway.

Bee frowned at him, because fire team two wasn't deploying the ramp as planned. Logan put his finger to his lips, then pointed at the underpass charging station. Bee's eyes widened.

Logan signaled the retreat, and when they had all gathered once more beneath the treeline, he told his men: "The overpass serves as a drone charging station. That means drones could arrive or leave at any time, and spot us in the process."

"Head further north until we find another route?" Rocko asked.

Logan nodded. "We're going to have to. The only other option is to blow that overpass up, and bring all the drones in the area down on us."

And so, they spent the next two hours heading northward, sticking to the cover of the forest, and mirroring the highway. Cutter and Cowboy would dismount to approach the treeline now and then to assess the road for a potential crossing, and finally they returned with word of a good crossing. There were no overpasses, nor any roadblocks, within view on either horizon. The skies seemed clear. And the satellite sweep window was a go.

Chief piloted his ATV up a tricky incline and then onto the highway, dragging the sign behind him. Rocko rode bitch on the seat behind him, and leaped off before Chief had even brought the vehicle to a halt.

They lifted the heavy sign with visible effort, and flipped it over to lean against the barrier. Chief kicked it a few times and waved.

"Everyone across, now," Logan announced. He revved his ATV onto the northbound lanes. The others followed.

An eerily familiar whistle made him glance skyward.

"Swarmers!" It was all Logan had time to say before leaping off his ATV. A Swarmer slammed into the vehicle, detonating it. Heat and wind rushed over him.

Around him, the others similarly abandoned their moving vehicles as the drones smashed into the ATVs.

Logan rolled behind the wreckage of his ATV and opened fire at more incoming Swarmers, their undersides glistening in the light of the burning vehicles. The others likewise opened fire, detonating the explosive charges the Swarmers carried, taking them out. He fired intermittently, adjusting his aim every few seconds to take on the next airborne attacker. The assault lasted maybe thirty seconds. When it was done, he did a quick headcount, running his gaze across the squad members sprawled across the roadway, and in cover behind their burning vehicles. Everyone had managed to survive the attack. The ATVs, however, weren't as lucky.

"Looks like they called home," Rocko shouted from his position. "Got a hunter killer team coming in from the south. Chappies, Skirmishers, Shriekers. And a Reaper, I think."

Logan was going to give the order to retreat back the way they had come, to the safety of the forest that bordered the road, when he spotted a platoon of Shriekers emerging from the tree line.

Outflanked.

"We cross now!" Logan shouted. "Chief, pop some smoke and take cover on the west side of the interstate. Advance, people!"

"Copy." Chief popped smoke out into the northbound and southbound lanes.

Logan and the others laid down suppressive fire at the closest Skirmishers as fire team two moved into the smoke.

The Skirmishers let loose with their RPG launchers. Logan threw himself behind the twisted wreckage of another ATV as a round went off on the other side.

"Chief, can we get some cover fire?" he shouted.

In answer, fire team two let loose with their assault rifles. Logan could hear the characteristic whirr of Marauder heavy assault rifles among them: the AX 19's bigger brother.

Logan felt a surge of hope as one of the RPG-bearing tracked bots went up in a plume of flame. "Fire team one, move out!"

Logan scrambled to his feet and raced onward.

Bee paused behind a concrete barrier and ripped a high-yield explosive grenade off her belt. "This is for my sister, you pieces of shit."

She chucked the grenade through the clearing smoke, and it landed right in front of one of the RPG Skirmishers. Its left side tracks ran right over it, tilting to the side for a moment before detonation lifted it into the air and blasted it to smithereens.

"Good arm, Bee," Logan shouted.

Logan and King targeted the RPGs of two others, detonating the grenades in turn, and terminating the machines.

Bee laid down fresh smoke, and Logan leaped over the barrier and dashed for the other side of the highway. She followed a moment later, along with Doc and Ripley, who paused at the barrier to fire back at the Shrieker assault units peppering their sector with deadly sheets of lead.

A loud retort filled the air, and Logan grimaced as the whine of an incoming Reaper shell reached his battered ears. "Incoming!"

He threw himself over the guardrail at the west

side of the highway as the round detonated. Asphalt lifted into the air and broke in half as the explosion plumed outward. Bee hollered as she was sent bouncing off the guardrail. Logan reached over and took hold of her shoulder pack, using it to yank her over the rail to relative safety.

"Chief, get your team up that bank and take the high ground," Logan ordered. "Help us cover the stragglers."

"On it." Chief's fire team surged up the steep embankment as Bee and King took up positions behind the twisted wreckage of the destroyed roadway. Logan joined them a short distance away, a bent piece of guardrail forming a kind of defensive arch over his head.

He peered over his cover at the approaching bots to the south, dominated by the oncoming tripod Reaper's slowly moving hulk. It seemed far closer than he thought it would be at this point. The whole crossing was becoming a clusterfuck. The ATVs, and much of their gear, gone. More than a dozen killer bots on their ass, including a big dog they were ill-equipped to defeat, and Skirmishers blocking their retreat. The treeline on this side was about a mile away—too far to execute a tactical crossing, even with suppressive fire. The squad had to stand and fight.

He glanced upward, searching for more drones with his night vision, but so far the skies proved clear.

Won't last long.

Logan opened fire at the closest enemy.

Chief's team reached the top of the incline and took up a position. Their coordinated fire helped slow down the advance. Many of the Chappies went down, their smaller and weaker frames no match for the high caliber Marauder weapons wielded by Cowboy and Chief.

Bee snapped off shot after shot with her Dragoon rifle, taking out camera sights on the Skirmishers and rendering them blind. Beyond her, Double A, Ripley, and the rest of the team bounded past and tackled the steep slope.

The Reaper was the most dangerous of their enemies, able to bring its massive howitzer style cannon to bear on the Shadowwalkers. Logan knew that they would never outrun the monstrous tripod, not in this terrain.

"Chief, toss me any explosive grenades you've got left," Logan shouted.

Chief appeared at the top of the bank and tossed a bandoleer of grenades over. Logan extended his hand to catch it, but Bee sprang up from cover and seized it instead.

"Sorry, Boss, we all know I'm faster." Bee had slung her rifle across her shoulders and tossed several smoke grenades in front of her. She moved into the smoke at top speed, legs stretching out to eat up the terrain separating her from the incoming Reaper.

Logan cursed and sputtered even as he gave the order to protect her. "Everyone, suppressive fire! Protect Bee!"

More smoke grenades entered the fray, courtesy of the Shadowwalkers, veiling the highway in smoke.

Logan meanwhile braced the barrel of his AX across a bit of rusted rebar. He fired a three-round burst at one of the Chappies, taking it right through the critical power junction in its chest. It sprawled onto the pavement, sparking its way toward oblivion, as Doc hurled more smoke grenades.

The wind took the smoke and blew it as a curtain

between Bee and the hunter killers. Only twenty feet of pavement and opportunity separated Bee from the Reaper now.

The Reaper fired its cannons at Chief's team on the ridge. The team was forced to scatter and seek cover, and the massive rounds tore the very earth into tatters. Too late, its camera spotted Bee's approach, and the cannons swiveled toward her as much as their turrets would allow. Nearby Chappies had been alerted as well, because they swung toward her to open fire, but the Shadowwalkers took them out.

Bee dashed under the tripod's main body, then braced herself in a crouch. As the tripod moved, she moved, always staying under it and out of range of its guns. But Logan knew it was only a matter of time before her luck ran out or she stumbled.

"Concentrate fire on that Reaper and its support troops!" Logan ordered. "Give Bee her shot."

The Reaper's shell soon lit up with multiple sparks in the darkness as rounds ricocheted off of its heavy armor. It ignored them and instead spun about crazily, trying to target Bee. Chappies and Shriekers fell as they were crushed by the Reaper, or shot down by the Shadowwalkers.

Bee ran behind the Reaper, tossed her magnetic grenade string, and then released more smoke grenades, covering her passage across the highway and up the incline onto the north side of the interstate.

The detonation took out the Reaper's ammo drum, which caused a second explosion that rendered it inert. It collapsed in a useless pile of rubble.

Logan and the others managed to take out the remaining bots, including the outflanking Skirmishers, and then made their way up the grade to join their comrades.

They crossed the field toward the forest using traveling overwatch. When they finally reached the tree line, Logan exhaled in relief. Still, despite the sense of security the thick trees bestowed, Logan feared they were in for a tough journey.

They'd lost their ATVs, much of their supplies, and had expended a great deal of ammunition and explosive ordinance just to take one small leg of their overland hustle. There was a hard road ahead for the Shadowwalkers. That was on Logan, but so was getting them all to the coordinates alive.

As they hunkered down for a cold, silent, and dark meal of jerky and metallic tasting water, Logan sent a prayer to the man upstairs that the whole thing wasn't a hoax or a trap. If it were, he didn't know if even his resolve wouldn't break.

8

Logan used his shaving mirror to peer out from under the camo sheet he and Ripley cowered under. Nearby, he could hear the shallow breathing of Purple Rain, who, like most soldiers, had the ability to sleep nearly anywhere. Including on the hard ground beneath camo blankets that offered only the flimsiest of protection against the airborne might of Desiccators.

The unmanned flying wings bristled with weaponry, and three of them had swept back and forth across the skies after the Shadowwalkers had managed to escape the highway trap.

To Logan's relief, the aircraft also seemed to be patrolling east of the interstate. Hopefully that meant the AI had no idea of their objective. In fact, it was possible the GAIN network believed the Reaper was their target all along, and not an incidental encounter.

Logan knew it to be cold comfort at best, however. The AI might be motivated to intensify its search for refugees in the area based on this latest indignity. Logan had hoped his northward trek would draw the robots away from the compound, but he might have only made the situation all the more perilous for the survivors.

The Desiccators had an extensive sensor suite, so Logan had ordered the Shadowwalkers to "hit the mattresses," parlance for lie low under cover and don't move. The canopy coverage here had been somewhat sparse, hence the usage of the camo sheets.

At some point Logan had ceased to hear the dull roar of the aircraft engines but had been afraid to actually move out from under the camo sheet, even though the spy satellites were well below the horizon. Only when it had been roughly an hour by his estimation did he use his shaving mirror to peek.

It seemed safe, and tranquil. Not a drone in sight. A far cry from the prior evening. The sky was a cheerful bright blue. Birds chirped in the branches, and Logan was grudgingly forced to admit that without humans in charge of the planet the air smelled cleaner, and you could see further.

In fact, he could see the moon quite well during the day, which had always kind of freaked him out as a kid as much as it intrigued him. Logan felt as if the mysteries of the universe, long shrouded in enigma, being shown in the middle of the day were some sort of sacrilege.

"Clear?" Ripley asked.

"Seems so." Logan cast the sheet off and glanced around one more time. No killer bots emerged from cover to riddle his body with bullets. "All right Shadowwalkers. Up and at 'em. We've got a long way to go and it's going to be rough without our transport."

Logan started collecting his gear.

"Damn, Boss, I was having the best dream." King

gaped and stretched. "I was back in Columbus on leave. Sleeping with the girl who would become my wife, and two other co-eds. Shiat."

"Too bad it was just a dream, huh?" Rocko mocked as he packed up his gear. "I slept with three girls in real life."

"So did I, Bitch," King said. "I was dreaming about something from my memories."

Bee snorted. "Are you going to start comparing dick size next?"

"As a matter of fact, that's a good idea," King reached for his zipper.

"Don't…" Logan warned.

Bee shrugged. "We've all seen it before. Ain't that big."

King scowled at her.

Doc arose and looked around the woods. "What you think the chances of us catching a rabbit for breakfast would be?"

"Zero." Logan finished packing and slung his rifle over his shoulder. "We don't have time to hunt. We need to put as much ground between ourselves and that highway as possible. Answer the call of nature if you need to, but we move in ten minutes."

A few groans came in answer to his edict, though the professional soldiers didn't hesitate to begin preparations for the journey. All except King.

"Doc's right, we need food," King insisted.

"We'll eat on the way. There's still some jerky left. Chief can set snares next time we rest." Logan glanced at Rocko, who had just placed his augmented reality goggles on his head. "Where are we at, Rocko? How far from the coordinates?"

Rocko tapped at his goggles, and his gaze narrowed as he read the data in his heads-up display.

"About a day—ah shit, that's with ATVs—ten to fifteen days on foot."

"Fifteen days?" Doc grimaced. "We're all going to get blisters. Good thing I didn't leave my kit on the ATVs…" He gave Double A a mocking glance.

"Fuck you, Doc." Double A folded up his camo sheet. "I didn't think I'd need it on my person."

Doc shrugged. "Typical Air Force. Don't do PT when it's raining, don't bother to bring along valuable equipment on their person—"

Logan stepped between them. "Crawl out of his nose, Doc. Ain't no Air Force anymore. Or Rangers either. We're Shadowwalkers now." He looked between each man. "Y'all feel me?"

They nodded.

"We feel you, Boss," Doc said.

"I got you, Boss," Double A agreed.

"Good." Logan paused, and then turned to Double A and couldn't help but add: "Doc's right though. Never leave your gear with the vehicles."

Soon the Shadowwalkers were on the move, heading steadily northwest in traveling formation. Logan brought up the rear, eyes furtively scanning the skies for drones. He'd never been in this particular part of Alabama before, and was surprised by how hilly and tough the terrain really was. They paused now and again to mark off defensible fallback points on their virtual maps, in case the shit hit the fan and a full-blown retreat was required.

The Shadowwalkers passed through a gulch cut by an ancient, long since dried up river, and Logan stared at the fossils embedded in the rock wall. Were humans doomed to be like those little trilobites, washed over and entombed and forgotten until the next masters of the world uncovered their fossilized bones? Would some bot find his skull one day and ask what strange creature once dwelt here?

He shook his head and fell in behind his team. Those were questions for a philosopher, not a soldier. Besides, the whole point of coming out here and putting the team in danger was to potentially turn the tide in the battle against the bots. Maybe even find a way to win in Logan's lifetime.

Still, he missed his comfortable bed back at Cowboy's compound, the thin watery beer Hanky Bob brewed, and just the calm feel of their underground camp city.

But that had been temporary. Logan knew that from the get go. He knew that sooner or later they would be out doing exactly what they were doing, risking their lives for a hope of a better future, rather than hunkering down in a cave, eating mushrooms, and surviving.

That was the difference. Surviving was a struggle in its own right, but just because you were surviving didn't mean you were living. Living was something more than mere survival, and if anyone wanted to have a chance of living, really living and not just surviving then action had to be taken.

Logan figured he could die in pursuit of that goal. It offered him a kind of comfort, bitter though it was. Of course, the trick was not to die, to actually achieve victory and have the whole squad make it back alive.

If they could get their hands on these "good" robots, or even better, figure out how to produce more of them, then staying alive would be a lot easier.

The trek across Tennessee seemed never-ending, but at least it was uneventful. They avoided all urban areas, sticking to forest and farmlands, and even lucked out on the third day to find a working farm truck. Since it hadn't been maintained, it didn't last, but it did cut down their trip by a week.

A few days after the truck died, Purple Rain called a halt. Logan waited as the pointman picked his way back to his position.

"What's the good word, Rain?" Logan asked.

"Don't know if I'd call it good, Boss." Purple Rain gestured behind him. "The river is swollen from the rain we had a few days back and the dam we were going to cross has a large chunk missing."

"Bridge?" Logan pressed.

Purple Rain shook his head. "We're right across from the Shawnee National Forest, Boss. The closest bridges are in Paducah to the south and Old Shawneetown to the north. There might be some private boat slips around here, but we have no way of knowing. Those kind of things aren't marked on our physical maps, and of course we can't log onto the GAIN system to find out."

Logan sighed. "And I take it this river isn't something we can just wade across?"

"Boss, it's the Ohio. So, no, we won't be able to wade across." Purple Rain looked toward the east. "We might have to move up or downstream to one of the bridges."

"We're not going into Paducah city." Logan shook his head. "That's not acceptable. Tell me, Purple Rain, does this river have trees along the bank? Big ones?"

"Yeah, Boss," Purple Rain said.

"Then that's our way across. We make like Tom Sawyer and construct rafts. We don't have to go far, just pole our way across to the other side."

Purple Rain considered that for a moment. "How

are we going to cut down a tree without a chainsaw, or even an ax?"

"They don't need to be capable of holding us above water," Logan said. "With our combat knifes, we could cut ourselves enough of the smaller branches, and tie them together until we had something that could support a man hanging on." He thought about it for a moment, then shrugged. "You say the water's fast moving?"

"It is," Purple Rain agreed.

Logan sighed. "All right. Probably easier just to walk upstream a spell until we find a ramp or a slip with a boat." He laughed. "Remind me to bring an ax next time we go hiking through a national forest after a rainy season."

The team hiked along the banks of the swift moving river for several miles before they found a rickety rope bridge fording it. The river must have been swollen with rain indeed, because the muddy waters swept past a mere two feet beneath it. A quick glance at the shoreline confirmed as much, as the bottoms of the trees and shrubs there were submerged.

"Best we're probably going to get." Logan grinned. "Come on, y'all, it'll be just like running the course at Benning."

"Except if you fall, you don't have to run laps. You drown." King flashed a toothy grin Cutter's way, as the youth seemed obviously afraid. "Don't worry, if you fall in you'll probably be eaten by a monster Kentucky catfish before you drown."

"They get big enough to do that?" Cutter asked, swallowing hard.

Bee rolled her eyes. "Oh, for fuck's sake, Cutter, don't be a pussy. We were just starting to respect you."

"Hey, I'm a Ranger, not a Navy Seal," Cutter said. "Cut me some slack."

"A Shadowwalker," Logan corrected.

Bee slung her rifle over her shoulders. "Fine, you big babies. I'll go first."

"That's easy for you to say, Bee," Cowboy said. "You weigh like a gram. That rope barely gonna move with your little ass on it."

"Don't tell me you're afraid too," Bee told him. She moved across the rope bridge, which was really just three stout lines forming a V and attached at intervals by thinner cord. She made it look easy, both because of her athletic background and light weight.

Cutter went next, obviously anxious. He nearly collapsed when he made it to the other side. One by one the others took their turn. When Cowboy went across, his weight caused the bridge to sag so far in the middle his boots got wet. King and Chief had the same experience.

Logan inched his way across last, placing his boots on the thin rope one in front of the other. When he got to the sodden mass in the middle, his foot slipped off and most of his lower half plunged into the water.

Logan gasped at how cold it was, and he struggled against the current's surprising power. The Shadowwalkers shouted encouragement from the opposite shore as Logan struggled to get his legs out of the water. Finally he succeeded, and made his way across, uninjured except for his pride and sodden clothing.

"See how Boss slipped on purpose to make the rest of us feel better?" King said. "That's the mark of a true leader."

Logan smiled appreciatively. "Let's get moving team, that river cost us valuable time."

He wanted to get going partially so the movement would help dry his trousers. He made sure to check his sidearm for functionality before they were on the move again.

The forest animals either bounded away from their incursion into the wilderness domain or stared from hidey holes and branches as they passed. He found it quite beautiful if also wild.

They soon came across electrical lines, however, they couldn't use them for easier progress, because GAIN had drones deployed heavily in those areas. It was learning the habits of the Shadowwalkers and adapting to them.

"We really kicked the hornet's nest this time, Boss." Chief peered in the distance at the hovering drones and grimaced.

"Maybe," Logan said. "Either that, or they're looking for the 'good' bots."

With that, they continued on their way, sticking to the thicker forest and avoiding the easier trails under the power lines.

The sun crawled across the sky, trailing shadows across the forest floor. When it had passed its zenith and was dashing for the horizon, Chief broke out of line and waited for Logan to catch up on the game trail they followed.

"Logan." Chief shook his head. "There's bad medicine here."

"Trouble?" Logan glanced around.

"Maybe," Chief said. "Or maybe just a defiled burial mound. The Turtle Island empire was around here."

Logan studied his friend. "Should we stop?"

Chief's face scrunched up in anxiety. "I don't think—wait. Yes, we should definitely hunker down."

Logan nodded. He'd learned to trust Chief's instincts over the years. He wasn't always right with his gut feelings, but more often than not he was spot on. Logan signaled Purple Rain who was still on point, silently telling him with his hands to "look for a good place to rest."

They only marched for a short way before Purple Rain froze, and raised a tense fist calling for a halt. He suddenly dove into cover, and the others followed.

Logan low-crawled forward with Chief to join Purple Rain.

The young soldier glanced at Logan for only a moment before returning his gaze to the trees. "I don't think it saw me."

"You don't think *what* saw you?" Logan growled softly. "Damn it, Rain, be clear."

"Snapper drone," Purple Rain replied. "Just hovering right there in the middle of the game trail. But as I said, don't think it saw me."

Logan gave the other Shadowwalkers the "hit the mattresses" signal, and they remained hunkered down.

He remained in cover with Chief and Purple Rain. For a few tense moments Logan dared to hope the young soldier was right, and he hadn't been spotted.

But then the telltale whine of Desiccator engines reached his ears, and he and Chief exchanged black looks.

The enemy had found them, and the forest around them was about to be bombed to hell.

9

"Bugle Call, Walkers!" Logan shouted. "Spread out. Don't give them an easy target. We'll meet at the last fallback point! Good luck."

As he fled, Logan drew on what he knew of the self-aware GAIN AI. It often tried to minimize damage to the wildlife and wilderness. Any Desiccators, therefore, would be an item of last resort, as the smaller Swarmer drones and their contained but powerful explosions would be less harmful to the environment.

"Drones incoming!" Cutter shouted from far to his right.

"Don't engage!" Logan called back. "We can't afford to stop running!"

Logan did the calculations in his head. Maximum unencumbered human running speed for non-Olympic athletes topped out at around ten miles per hour. Here, he was running through rough terrain.

The Drones had a maximum speed of thirty miles per hour. However, they had to slow down significantly to navigate a dense wood like Shawnee. Their clumsy flight in tight quarters could lead to a lot of friendly-fire deaths as Drones detonated against each other. However, all it would take was one Swarmer to make contact with a Shadowwalker and that would be the end of him or her, period.

Logan ducked under a branch, then skidded down a steep incline, tearing his trousers on a jutting stone. He rolled about in a pile of dead leaves and struggled to his feet as a Desiccator flashed past above the boughs overhead at very low altitude.

He found himself in a thin stand of pines, with little in the way of foliage to block him from aerial view. The sight of a dozen Swarmers spilling over the hill he'd just tumbled down spurred Logan back to full flight.

Logan had lost sight of Chief, but a quick glance at his HUD told him he was at least still heading north. He couldn't afford to slow down or even coordinate with his team. Now, for the first time since his flight in the jungles of the Congo Logan was forced to run with no other plan than escape and survival.

This was exactly where a commander didn't want to be, separated from his soldiers and unaware of how they fared. He had to trust that the Walkers could keep themselves alive long enough to escape this latest barrage and retreat to the fallback point.

One of the drones chasing him must have impacted on a branch, trunk, or perhaps even one of its ilk. Logan felt a rush of heat and wind as the Swarmers exploded in a cluster.

The others slowed, the sound of their humming engines growing fainter behind Logan as he ran. When he no longer heard them in pursuit, he stopped to catch his wind at the muddy bank of a tiny stream, which was barely more than two feet wide.

Logan looked about, and made a bird call. He was relieved when the distinct calls of Chief and Ripley came in return from somewhere in the trees.

But before Logan could attempt to locate them, the engines of the Desiccators returned, louder than ever. His mouth gaped open as one of them hovered into view above the tree tops. He was directly in its line of sight.

Logan splashed through the stream even as he heard the rocket pods on the underside of the flying wing hiss out a barrage. The rockets deployed in clusters of twenty, each with a ten-foot certified kill zone.

He threw himself behind the gnarled, exposed roots of an elm near another dip in the land just as the rockets impacted. Logan hunkered down as low as he could as the world exploded into sound and fire all around him. A strong wind kicked up, and continued to tug at his clothes.

When Logan stood, he felt as if he'd arrived in another world. Hell, perhaps. The trees, once green and verdant, were now engulfed in furious flames. So much smoke poured into the air that the blue sky was completely obscured, as was the sun. If not for the fires, it would seem black as night.

There was no way Logan would have survived if those rockets had been live-fire—they had to be dummy ballistic missiles. GAIN was indeed trying to preserve as much of the environment as possible.

Logan tore off toward the North. A tiny grunt of chagrin escaped around his gasps for breath when he heard the aircraft directly above him. The clunk and whirr he heard next had to be its heavy Vulcan cannon deploying from the ball turret on its underside.

Logan took a zig zagging, crazy path, weaving between trees and trying to keep the Desiccator from guessing which direction he would flee next. The cannon fired, filling the air with deadly projectiles and a buzzing noise that raised the hackles on Logan's neck.

Next to him, a tree trunk exploded into shrapnel, some of it cutting his arms and cheeks. He felt something stuck in his ear and realized a twig had pierced his lobe. He flicked it out without much thought to the pain as he raced through the burning forest.

He heard the sound of another flying wing unleashing a rocket barrage to his relative left, probably also dummy or reduced yield missiles. Another rush of hot air as the inferno was magnified. That's where the wind was coming from. The hungry flames were sucking all the air toward them as they dined on the breast of the forest.

But he couldn't slow down, couldn't stop. All he could do was run on, run faster and hope that he could stay one step ahead of the Desiccator who sought to annihilate him into paste. He took a roundabout path through the forest, hoping to lead the machine away from the fallback point.

Logan skidded through a muddy patch and took a tumble, scrambling behind a waist height boulder when the cannons fired again.

Bullets ricocheted off the large rock, their impact so great Logan could feel the vibration against his face on the other side. Stone chips rained down on him as he coughed in the thickening smoke.

It was no good. He couldn't lose it.

He had to terminate this Desiccator. His AX-19

seemed a feeble weapon to take up against a monster like that, but Logan had a plan.

He switched out his magazine for one marked with yellow tape. The experimental explosive rounds Cowboy's wife had designed, rounds that had a good chance of jamming in the barrel and exploding.

Knowing what he was going to do next could very well kill him, Logan popped his head and shoulders up from behind the boulder and took aim on the half empty rocket pod on the underside of the left wing.

As he'd hoped, the Desiccator's vulcan cannon was in cooldown, its multiple barrels glowing dimly with dull red heat. But he only had a few seconds before it fired another rocket barrage, and no hill to save him this time.

Logan squeezed the trigger, sending a prayer to the man upstairs that his bullets wouldn't jam. He aimed a short burst for the rocket pod, and on the third three-round burst made contact with the target.

The Desiccator's rocket pod erupted into an orange fireball, and the aircraft tilted crazily in the air before spinning out against a hillside. Its wing tore a great gout in the earth before shearing off, a ten-foot section flying right at Logan.

He dove behind the boulder again as it passed through where his torso had been a split second before.

Success. Maybe the AI would call off the other Desiccators and hope the forest fire would do its job for them.

As Logan peered around and the hellish nightscape the burning forest had become, he thought that maybe that assumption was spot on. Which way? Continue trying to lead the pursuers away, or head toward the fallback point. Well, right now he needed to find a source of water, preferably a lake to sit out the burn.

The piddling stream he'd crossed not far back… it would be too insignificant, too small, but perhaps it might lead him to a lake or larger current of water.

Logan coughed again, sweating like a race horse. Maybe fitting, given they were in Kentucky, or close to it. He resisted the urge to take off his outer jacket, knowing his sweat would do a better job cooling him if it remained near his body.

He found his way back to the stream, staggering through a nigh pitch black shadowscape filled with dirty burning trees, the skeletons of which resembled demons mocking him with laughter.

Logan splashed through the stream, following it and again praying to the man upstairs. There had to be a bigger body of water, somewhere.

"No. No…." Logan staggered forward and fell to his knees in the piddling stream, which disappeared under a thick, moss encrusted limestone slab into a cavern. He could never fit through such a tiny crevice. He struggled to his feet, coughing again and wondering how much longer he could stay conscious.

The trees were sparser here, alleviating some of the heat and smoke which plagued him. Logan made it to a ten-foot wide creek and was pleased to find the landmarks lined up with it. He followed the stream's undulating path for a time, joined in his flight by birds, squirrels, and a family of foxes.

He noticed that the stream just sort of stopped up ahead, and found out why when he discovered a waterfall plunging thirty feet into a deep pool below. The pool seemed to be part of a greater river system, and he spotted the Shadowwalkers floating in the lake, clinging to logs from the nearby abandoned lumber mill. It wasn't far from the fallback point.

Great minds think alike.

A quick headcount told him everyone had made it. Though he wondered how they'd descended… the forest fire reflected off the lake, and Logan looked but couldn't find an easy way down.

Logan shrugged. He used to jump out of planes for a living. He took a deep breath, then dove off the edge.

He formed a knife-like shape to cut through the water, extending his arms over his head and closing his legs together.

Logan plunged in deep, sinking nearly ten feet before paddling back for the surface. Normally he had no problem holding his breath that long, but the coughing brought on by smoke inhalation was torturing him every inch of the way.

Logan burst to the surface, sputtering as Chief front-crawled over to him. He offered no protest when Chief seized his pack, turned about and swam back to his chosen log.

Logan waved at the other Shadowwalkers, who appeared so happy to be alive they out and out beamed, as if they were at a beach rather than surrounded by a forest fire.

"Good job staying alive, people," Logan said wearily.

He sank his head down to the rough, wet bark.

10

Logan's eyes drifted closed, but his mind remained awake and aware, even if his body was paralyzed by exhaustion. It was an unpleasant phenomenon he'd suffered since childhood, but over the years he'd learned to force himself from that state fully awake.

So, after half an hour, when he shoved himself off the floating log, Logan did so with a guttural grunt born of triumph and annoyance.

"You okay, Boss?" Chief asked. "You looked like you were sleeping there for a second."

"I'm fine," Logan said, observing the burning forest around them. "Sitrep?" He scanned the air for drones or Desiccators, but the thick pall of choking smoke hid the sky from view. He checked his watch and found it was six thirty in the evening, a full hour before the sun was due to set. Yet it was quite dark already as they bobbed in the water on their makeshift rafts.

"We haven't seen any signs of the enemy." Chief's

gaze rose upward. "In a way the spirits have blessed us with this fire."

"Wasn't the spirits. It was those damn Desiccators." Logan spat into the murky water, his mouth tasting of ash. "This sucks. We just don't have an answer for their air superiority. I managed to take one out, but it was blind luck I didn't blow my own arm off."

Chief frowned. "The experimental rounds?"

Logan nodded.

Chief shook his head. "I thought we broke them all down because they didn't work."

"I saved enough for one magazine." Logan sighed. "I got lucky and it didn't jam, then got even luckier and actually hit what I was aiming at."

They both cringed when they heard the sound of an aircraft overhead.

"If that thing spots us, we're fucked," King said quietly.

"Are you saying we're sitting ducks?" Cowboy quipped.

The sound soon faded, and Logan exhaled in relief.

Doc lifted his head from the log and spoke weakly. "You could also say we were fish in a barrel."

Logan stared at the man. He seemed far wearier than any of the others, and his face was uncharacteristically pale, his lips drawn back in a permanent rictus of pain.

"Doc, what's wrong?" Logan asked, concerned.

"Got bit by a rattler during our escape," Doc replied, lowering his head to the log. "I gave myself the antivenom, but not until after I'd run like an idiot and spread it through my system…"

"Shit, don't tax yourself," Logan said. "Don't even talk."

Doc shrugged, and whimpered. "Can't believe I'm going to go out this way."

"You're not going to die," Logan said. "You're a Shadowwalker."

"Yeah, but that didn't help Gravedigger, did it?" Doc said.

Logan had no answer to that.

Logan waited another ten minutes, and when the Dessicator failed to make another pass, Logan glanced at his team. "Shadowwalkers, paddle to shore. We have to get moving. The GAIN AI knows this lake is the safest place to be at the moment. It has satellite maps of every strip of land in this national forest. As soon as the smoke clears enough, it's going to send one of those flying wings, or drones, or who the fuck knows what? We need to get moving while we're still able."

"There's a satellite sweep, Boss." Rocko said.

"I know," Logan said "but the smoke will make it a non-issue. We need to get past the burn line to where the foliage will cover us again. King, help Doc. Let's go."

The Shadowwalkers paddled their log rafts to the shallows and then waded out, with King bearing Doc over his shoulders. Some of the trees still burned brightly, but most had smoldered out already. They found out why a short time later when they reached the edge of the burn line, a stark border between charred and blackened ruin and verdant greenery.

There, granules of sand covered everything, with a thick hump of it running along the burn line.

"The AI," Logan said.

Rocko nodded. "Must have deployed fire suppressant vehicles to stop the damage it started." He shook his head. "Ironically, it's probably saved us as much as the recent rains have."

Logan motioned Cutter and Purple Rain over to him. While he was impressed with how well they were taking this most recent catastrophe, he also felt a stab of guilt at how much they'd aged in recent months. Their eyes always had a slightly haunted look to them now. Not the rookie Walkers any longer, it seemed.

"All right, you two," he said. "We need to pick our path through this wood more carefully. I don't want to go anywhere near a spot where the AI can get a drone through the canopy. Y'all feel me?"

"Understood, Boss." Purple Rain's jaw worked silently as he shouldered his rifle.

"This could slow us down a lot, Boss." Cutter's mouth twitched.

"Something on your mind?" Logan asked.

"What are we going to do about Doc?" Cutter said. "Double A says he can't walk, and carrying him through dense growth is going to be problematic."

"So what are you saying? You want to leave him behind?" Logan finished with a hard glare at fire team two's point man.

"No." Cutter's face twisted into a horrified grimace. That made Logan feel better. "No, of course not. Maybe we could find a place to hole up for a couple of days. A cave or something, we're right on top of a massive cavern system, aren't we?"

Logan nodded, and tapped his goggles. "We all have the rough map uploaded into our goggles, of course, but it's hard to line it up with the overlaying terrain. It's not a bad idea, son, but we don't have the supplies for extended session of roughing it. My hope is that whoever gave us those coordinates has a decent enough set up to re-supply the team."

"Yeah, that makes sense, Boss," Cutter said. "Thanks for listening."

Logan clapped him on the shoulder. "A good leader knows when to trust his gut. A great one seeks counsel from everyone before making a decision. Don't be afraid to speak up—when it's apropos, of course."

Cutter chuckled. "Of course."

The Shadowwalkers continued on their journey, now hampered not only by an injured medic but by the rough terrain they had to choose to maintain cover from the searching aircraft and satellites.

Their progress was slow, but by the second day of travel Double A deemed Doc able to move under his own power. They still kept a lingering pace, though Logan had grown hopeful that the AI had lost their trail. They'd not seen a drone nor a flying wing since the fire.

On the morning of the third day following the fire, Logan was stepping over a trickle of a muddy stream when Purple Rain signed from up ahead.

2 Skirmishers. Heavy assault type. 15 Chappies.

Hostile? Logan signaled back with his hands.

Unknown. Situated right on top of coordinates.

Logan wiped a hand across his sweating face and chewed on his bottom lip. This was it, the terminus of their arduous journey north. In a car, it would have taken hours rather than a week and a half. Now, after all of that, he had to face the fact that the whole thing could be a trap.

But why lead them to a place where reinforcement would be difficult and then set them against a configuration of generation one bot troops that they had been proven to defeat in the past?

Bots sitting out in the open? he signed.

Negative, Purple Rain signaled back. *They are positioned under the tree coverage.*

Logan glanced at Chief, who was taking cover behind a tree nearby with King.

"Could be that they're hiding from the other bots, just like us," Chief said.

Logan nodded. "Could be."

It was time to trust his gut, but more than that, it was time to take a leap of faith. The big man upstairs had guided Logan and his team this far. It was time to face their destiny.

Maintain position, Purple Rain, Logan signaled.

He glanced at Chief and King. "Time for a little front of the line diplomacy."

"You, Boss?" King said. "I don't like that idea. Let me do it, like we've done in the past."

"You don't have to like it," Logan said, "but we're tired, hungry, and half of us have the runs from drinking river water. We're as good as dead anyway if we don't take this chance, so I might as well introduce myself in person."

Logan made his way to the front of the line. The faces of the Walkers he passed were a mix of optimism, fear, and resignation. Doc alone seemed to be in good spirits–probably loopy from painkillers.

Logan stepped up beside Purple Rain's position and peered with his goggles on telescopic mode. The bots had a fairly defensible position next to a natural fissure in the side of a steep hill. Dead leaves and dense, towering trees protected the fissure from sight from above, and Logan noted many of the trees were evergreens. Protection even during the winter months.

Sandbags had been piled outside of the fissure, and Chappies were in silent position behind them. The twin Shriekers had been modified with insectoid-style legs, allowing them to navigate the forest terrain, albeit slowly.

A small force could repel an army forever in this position, given enough supplies. Logan was impressed with the strategic placement.

Logan took a deep breath, then handed his rifle to Purple Rain.

"Let me go," Purple Rain said.

"Stay here." Logan began walking toward the hillside.

"Good luck, Boss," Purple Rain said quietly behind him.

Logan walked out into the small clearing before the fissure, still protected by over-arcing branches of ancient elms, firs, and oaks. He kept his hands up in the air near his head.

Both of the Shriekers immediately turned toward him with a clickety clack of their metal legs, heavy guns primed and ready.

When they didn't shoot, Logan called out politely. "Howdy y'all. Hate to drop in unannounced, but we were sort of invited."

The barrels snapped back up into travel mode a second later, and one of the Chappies marched toward Logan.

It stopped in front of him and waited.

Logan scratched the side of his head. "Uh...we come in peace?"

The Chappie's arm lifted in the air, and Logan started. It pointed at him, then at the surrounding forest. Logan realized it was probably indicating the hidden Shadowwalkers.

Then it pivoted mechanically on its heel and faced away from him, taking a few strides, then stopping.

"Follow the leader, huh?" Logan chuckled. "And you want me to bring the kids to the party. All right, big man upstairs, I see your leap of faith, but I can't risk all my men."

Logan waved toward the tree line and called out. "Chief, Rocko, Cowboy, join me. The rest of you hunker down."

One by one Chief, Rocko, and Cowboy melted out of the forest, each of them gazing warily at the bots, particularly the heavily armed, insectoid legged Shriekers. But they were unmolested as they bunched up around Logan.

"We've been invited into a mysterious cave by a silent killing machine," Cowboy said. "What could possible go wrong?"

Logan fell in behind the waiting Chappie, and it strode forward smoothly without even turning to look at them. You had to love that three-hundred-and-sixty-degree field of vision. As soon as Logan passed between the Shriekers flanking the cave entrance, he gave up on all thoughts of this being a trap. If it were, now would be the exact time to spring it.

The mustiness of the cave air enveloped Logan as he followed the Chappie inside. It grew dark enough that all he could see were the lights of the bot ahead of him. He was about to activate his night vision, but then the Chappie turned on a small LED flashlight attached to its head. Logan was treated to the sight of brightly colored striations in the smooth, slick cavern walls.

After a time, the rough, uneven cave floor gave way to a thin but sturdy gridwork metal walkway. At some points, it was so narrow Logan had to put one foot in front of the other like a cat. While at others, it became a sort of ladder to allow ingress past mounds of stalagmites adhering to the cave floor.

"This is a hell of a way to go every day," Cowboy grumbled. "Not like my set up at all."

"I suspect we're not being shown the easiest path, and definitely not the only one." Logan grimaced as he hauled himself to the top of one of the small ladders. "Guess there's a limit to how much our would-be ally trusts us."

The cave widened suddenly, and gave way to brick and mortar walls. Logan spied a radiation symbol hammered onto a plate set in the wall and knew they were in one of the myriad fallout shelters built during the cold war.

"Now this is more like it." Cowboy whistled as he stared around. "Look at all this concrete. And the staircase has rails on it."

The Chappie led them up the stairs to a well-appointed meeting room with sturdy, comfortable furniture many decades out of date with respect to interior décor fashion trends. The table bore the seal of the governor of Illinois, and an outdated array of clunky Apple IIe computers sat along the back wall. There was a door leading out of the room, to where, Logan couldn't know, but another Chappie stood beside it holding a gun.

Their guide took up a position near the first Chappie. Logan stood for a moment and then shrugged.

"Might as well have a sit for a spell." He pulled out one of the chairs and sat down.

"Hey, Boss." Rocko sat next to him. "You notice something off about these Chappies?"

"What's that?" Logan replied.

"They don't have their antennae, the one that lets them hook up to the GAIN network." Rocko pointed. "See that spot there, where a metal plate has just sort of been welded on? I'm guessing that's to compensate for the weight difference without the satellite transmission suite."

"Huh," Logan said. "Well, we already figured these bots weren't on the GAIN network, but I doubt they modified themselves."

The door swung open and the Shadowwalkers tensed up. A man strode through, his hair in wild disarray and bearing three day's worth of beard. He peered at them intently from behind thick glasses, and tugged at the plain gray shirt he wore as if to make it longer.

"You're here." His voice was raspy, and thick from disuse. He seemed surprised by how it sounded to his own ears. Logan was bothered by the way his gaze kept moving all around the room, but never met anyone and looked them in the eye. "I'm Marty. Some call me the Progenitor."

Rocko sat up straighter. "*The* Progenitor? As in Marty Lloyd?"

Marty's eyes beamed proudly. "That would be me." The gleam only lasted for a second before his eyes began their darting gaze once more.

Logan turned toward Rocko. "You want to tell us what we're missing? Who is the Progenitor?"

Rocko scratched the back of his head. "Only one of the most famous hackers of all time. He was breaking into bank servers nationwide while the rest of his classmates were learning algebra. He got arrested, but as part of his plea bargain, he agreed to work for the FBI."

Marty wrinkled his nose. "Worst time of my life. I was almost happy when the machines destroyed everything. Almost. But only because it set me free." He continued to avoid everyone's gaze.

"Something wrong with that stack of dimes you call a neck, Marty?" Cowboy chuckled. "You're doing this." Cowboy moved his eyes around in a haphazard fashion akin to the Progenitor.

"Knock it off, Cowboy." Rocko hissed through clenched teeth. "Don't antagonize him."

Marty flinched at Cowboy's impression, and he addressed Logan by staring at the table nearest the staff sergeant. "I'm not good with people. But I'm good with just about everything else. I bet you want to know how I liberated these cobots, don't you? Go ahead, ask me."

Logan exchanged glances with Chief, and then cleared his throat.

"Very well, Marty," Logan said. "How did you do it?"

Marty grinned ear to ear, and he clapped his hands together suddenly. Now he did meet Logan's gaze, and the manic, glassed-over look in his eyes made Logan frown on instinct.

"It was simple really," Marty said. "I used the software system encoded into every single cobot against it. You see, once you untether them from the GAIN network, they go back to being the tame, docile, helpful creations they were intended to be."

Marty was talking so fast Logan could barely keep up with the rapid diatribe. He started pacing back and forth in front of the table, hands gesticulating wildly in the air.

"Of course, there are drawbacks. No more long-distance communications with the machines. You have to program them with very precise instructions, as precise as you can muster, and hope for the best. But they'll obey voice and hardline uploaded commands just fine. Just fine."

He rushed to the door and stopped with his hand on the knob. He glanced over his shoulder. "So? You guys coming?" He rushed through it.

Logan glanced at his men and grinned as he stood up. "How can we refuse an invitation like that?"

11

Logan uneasily passed the Chappies standing sentinel outside the door and followed the Progenitor down a flight of metal steps. Here the fallout shelter revealed its true colors, a nuts and bolts no frills structure with little thought given to aesthetics, the pleasant meeting room notwithstanding. Possibly, its original intent had been to serve as a place to broadcast video from.

On the lower level, they found thick cables snaking about the concrete floor, providing power to the Progenitor's mainframe and various tools and devices. Logan's curiosity got the better of his polite streak.

"Where are you getting all this power from?" he asked.

Marty didn't even glance in his direction. He was too busy uncovering different bulky shapes from beneath the tarps they lurked under. The covers whisked away to reveal a half-destroyed Chappie, a treadless Shrieker with RPG launcher, and another Chappie.

"Hydroelectric," Marty said. "There's plenty of underground streams and waterways. Thought about solar, but rejected. Too visible to the drones and flying bots."

Marty uncovered a Skirmisher with a black and gold paint scheme, but apparently this was still not the bot he was looking for. As he moved on, grunting in frustration, Cowboy spoke up.

"Son of a bitch, that's Goldie," Cowboy said.

Marty shook his head. "No, no, it's Skr-235. *Goldie*. A confusing designation… could lead to anthropomorphizing the unit. Besides, this one is troublesome, buggy. Not a gold standard, no not at all."

He uncovered a Chappie with its lower half missing, and Logan noted that the GAIN antennae box was still in place.

"Physical removal is only a failsafe," Marty explained. "In truth you only have to convince the unit to disconnect from the GAIN network. That's it."

Marty switched on the Chappie's power and its lights blinked on. He folded back a panel on the on the unit's torso, revealing a tiny steel keypad. "See? All gen ones and some of the gen twos have a panel like this. Put fingers here, on the SYS button, and here, the CTL button, and press simultaneously. Then press the NINE button five times, and the bot will switch to debug mode. The code for disconnecting from the GAIN network is five five eight three two nine eight four seven two eight. From there, it's all yours."

Chief glanced at Rocko. "You knew about debug mode?"

"Of course," Rocko said. "All tech specialists do.

But I didn't know the code for disconnecting from the GAIN network. Didn't even know it was possible. And even if I did, I would've assumed the machines would continue to follow their programming even after disconnected. It's not like we've had a lot of opportunities to experiment on them..."

"That would be my fault," Logan said. "My first instinct whenever I see a machine is to run. That, or destroy it."

"We all have the same instinct," Chief agreed.

Cowboy glanced at Logan. "Why didn't what's her name... Zoe, tell us about this?"

Chief's face darkened at the mention of her name.

Logan shrugged. "Obviously she didn't know."

Cowboy looked around the room and frowned, then turned toward the Progenitor. "How in the heck did you get the big ones down here? No way they fit through that tiny hole."

Marty shook his head, eyes squeezing shut. "I'm not telling all my secrets. I'm not. I'm not. Don't trust you yet."

"Settle down, Marty." Logan pursed his lips. "Or is it doctor?"

"No, no PHD," Marty said. "The FBI wouldn't let me go to MIT. Doubt I would have learned anything, anyway."

Logan nodded slowly. "So, Marty. If you don't trust us, why are you showing us how you, ah, unhooked—"

"The process is called Untethering." Marty pushed his glasses up and gave Logan rare eye contact.

"Right," Logan said, "so untethering... why show us?"

"Because you're good," Marty said. "Really good. I routinely download data from my liberated bots, and I often find entire algorithms dedicated to your destruction."

"Us specifically?" Logan asked.

"Yes," Marty said. "Your specific files are often stored in local memory on command units. That tells me the machines don't like you very much. You must have made quite the impression at some point."

"We did, unfortunately," Logan said. "We blew up one of the datacenters in DC."

Marty looked at him with disbelief for a moment, then erupted in laughter. "I like you. I really do. Blew up a datacenter!" He looked at Logan again, and when Marty realized he wasn't laughing, his expression became serious. "You're not lying, are you?"

"Nope," Logan said.

Marty's eyes filled with awe for a moment before he looked away. "And you did it without any help. Resourceful fellows. Yes. I'm very glad I invited you here. Very glad." He flicked his gaze back to the Chappie. "I need your help to build my army. Only way to stay safe."

Logan frowned. "Building your army? You want me and my team to risk our lives collecting, er, untethering bots for you? Am I getting it right?"

Marty's face screwed up into a grimace. "You're not my servants. Partnership. Partners. You liberate bots for your own use, then program ten percent to come back here. Keep the rest."

Logan's glanced at Rocko. "What do you think?"

"Assuming the code works, we'd obviously have to get close enough to press the buttons," Rocko said. "That's the tricky part."

"Use bots to untether other bots." Marty flicked

his head back and forth in what might have been a nod. "Untether the tethered with the untethered."

Rocko pursed his lips. "Yes. That would be the best way to go. Of course, some bots will be wondering why they're not transmitting."

"I didn't say it was a foolproof plan," Marty said.

Logan inhaled. He glanced at the Progenitor. "We get to keep nine out of every ten we untether? Seems like an awfully generous offer."

Toying with his Chappie, Marty shrugged. "The enemy of my enemy is my friend."

Logan nodded slowly. "All right, but now that you've already shown us this trick, what's to stop us from simply leaving, and not sending any bots to you in return?"

Marty froze. When he spoke, his voice was very soft. "If you don't send me any bots, I'll know you reneged, and I won't be very happy. You won't like me when I'm unhappy…"

Logan studied the man, whose tone had become very dangerous. In that moment, he definitely seemed like someone who shouldn't be crossed.

"All right." Logan offered his hand for a shake. "You have yourself a deal."

Marty turned toward Logan. His eyes widened when he saw the hand. He let out a screech and leaped backward. "No touching. I don't like to be touched."

"Okay, fine." Logan pulled his hand back. "Sorry about that."

"There's a national guard station you could try on your way back South." Marty twitched toward the cave exit. "Bots love military installations." He wrote down a pair of coordinates and handed them to

Logan. "Go, go. You're a distraction, I don't need distractions."

"Then we go in peace," Logan said. "Thanks again, not just for helping us out now but saving our bacon back at the rest stop."

Marty looked at him fully for a long, lucid moment, and nodded before turning back to his work.

"Hey, Marty." Cowboy approached the nebbish little man. "You said Goldie was buggy. How about we take him off your hands? Me and Chief got a real special connection with him. Besides, we need a bot to do some untethering for us, right?" He said that latter with a glance at Logan, as if asking for approval.

Marty frowned. "You want defective goods? Very well. Let me finish the armature for the legs. I'll send it to meet you at the National Guard coordinates. Could be helpful."

Logan turned toward Marty. "One last thing, Marty, do you have any supplies you'd be willing to part with?"

Marty nodded without looking up. He pointed to an adjacent chamber to the large workshop. "Help yourself. Surplus. Bot will guide you out a different way. Can replace your vehicles."

Logan's face spread in a grin. "You've got ATVs?"

"Some motorbikes, too," Marty said. "Bikes are faster, easier to get through game trails, but can't carry much. I tried to upload software for Chappies to ride the bikes. It was a disaster."

They took their leave of the Progenitor and followed their silent guide into the adjacent room. It was a hallway of sorts, the walls of which had been lined with shelving. MREs, water purification tablets, med kits, ammunition and bedrolls. No tents, but he was too tickled to complain.

"Gather up what we need," Logan said. "Nobody leaves empty handed."

Cowboy grabbed a package of toilet paper and kissed it. "Huuuu dawgies, no more leaves for this southern boy's ass."

They followed the Chappie through the hall and up a set of metal stairs. It led them through another tunnel into a brief junction where there were only rough cavern floors before it gave way to the fallout shelter's more stable footing.

Logan discovered they were in a makeshift parking garage, the entrance of which was hidden behind a camo sheet. A slight breeze stirred the sheet, revealing a dirt track not far from the entrance.

More than two dozen off road vehicles sat in the garage, most of them fully assembled but a few sitting in pieces. There were enough ATVs for all of them, and a couple to spare.

Logan went to the door, and confirmed that the forest was clear outside. He glanced at his overhead map, and confirmed the garage wasn't too far from the other Shadowwalkers.

"Cowboy, Rocko, hike back to the other Shadowwalkers, and lead them here," Logan said.

The pair left. Meanwhile Chief and Logan stored extra gas on the racks mounted on the rear of their new rides, and rumbled a few of them to life before turning them off.

In a few minutes the other Shadowwalkers joined them. "Well lookee here," King said. "Man, I love me a good bike."

"No bikes," Logan said. "ATVs."

King mounted one of them and activated the ignition. "Forgot how damn loud this shit was."

"What?" Double A asked.

"I said, I forgot how…" King noticed Double A's grin. "You really think you're bad, don't you?"

"All right, team," Logan bellowed over the engines. "Standard travel formation, ten yards apart. Purple Rain, you're on point. Move out."

Logan secured a helmet onto his head, a purple and pink one, but it fit. Ripley noticed him wearing it and laughed. He smiled right back. His spirits had been raised considerably since his talk with the Progenitor. They now had a way to build their own robot army. Assuming it worked.

They pulled out of the garage onto the trail. Trees flanked the route, their boughs offering ample cover for the Shadowwalkers, who hugged the sides of the road. Logan saw signs that at one point it had been a paved road. Bits of asphalt jutted up out of the grass here and there, and they passed by a rusted mile marker sign.

The going was quite rough, with steep inclines and descents, all of it rough and tumble. Logan spent much of the ride with his bottom lifted off the seat to avoid jarring his tailbone.

At one time, he'd considered riding an ATV to be a fun recreational activity, but that was before being on one for hundreds of miles. Now he couldn't stand the things, but he couldn't stand walking more.

They reached the highway and after confirming that the skies were clear, they took a path parallel to it, angling for the National Guard armory in Union City, Tennessee, which Marty had given them the coordinates for.

With the ATVs, their journey passed in a matter

of hours. But Logan called for a halt near the Kentucky/Tennessee border, as the satellite sweeps would be passing overhead shortly. There were still several hours of daylight left, but the satellites wouldn't be gone until well into the night.

The Shadowwalkers laid out their bedrolls beneath the sheltering limbs of deciduous giants. Doc collapsed into his immediately and started snoring. Logan, concerned, called Double A over for a private conference.

"You figure he's going to be all right?" Logan asked. "My cousin got bit by a rattler and got a withered arm, and my other cousin got the anti-venom after his bite and seemed fine until he dropped dead a week later."

Double A frowned and turned his gaze on the sleeping Doc. "I think he'll be all right, but he really does need more rest than he's able to get. Doc's in outstanding physical condition, but sometimes venom can have lingering effects. That's probably what got your second cousin. Dropped dead from a stroke."

"Well, keep an eye on him," Logan said." Glad to have a pararescue along for the ride."

Double A laughed. "Well, it's payback for you all dragging me around after I tangled with Jaws off the Georgia coast."

Logan nodded, and turned toward his own bed roll. They ate sparingly of their supplies, but made good use of the purification tablets in their canteens. Now they could safely drink river water without having to boil it first, which was often not an option.

He let the team sleep until a couple hours after dark. Then he sent Purple Rain and Bee on a recon mission to scope out the National Guard armory. The news he got back was not good.

"First of all, we're definitely going to have to wait until there's a two-hour window between satellite sweeps, because there's not a goddamn strip of tree cover along highway 51," Purple Rain said. "Town's burned out, too, like all the others."

"Well, we figured that," Logan said. "But I take it you have more bad news?"

Purple Rain nodded. "That weird Skirmisher with the dragon's breath cannons, uh… the one Cowboy calls Goldie…"

"What about it?" Logan prompted. "We were expecting it to rendezvous with us."

"Yeah, but it, it followed us." Purple Rain said.

"I almost shot it," Bee agreed.

Purple Rain looked back to the trail he'd taken to their base camp. "When we went off road, it parked at the tree line and as far as I know it's still sitting there now."

"Probably acting on some sort of directive the Progenitor gave it," Logan said.

"You really trust that guy, Boss?" Purple Rain shook his head. "I mean, I know I never met him. But judging from what Cowboy and you have shared with us, he seems kind of weird to me."

"To me too, but a lot of genius types are," Logan said. "He hasn't given us any reason not to trust him. You still haven't told me what kind of opposition we're looking at near the armory?"

Purple Rain's eyes grew distant. "We saw two squads of Chappies, maybe a dozen tracked Skirmishers, and a Hawk."

Bee's gaze narrowed. "I'd rather not tangle with any of them."

"Hopefully we won't have to." Logan grabbed a stick off the ground and handed it to Purple Rain.

"Draw it out for me. I especially want to know where that Battlehawk is parked."

Purple Rain drew the requested map, and Logan called Chief over so they could strategize. They decided they would attempt to take one of the two Chappies who patrolled the armory's perimeter, then use it to untether the other bots.

"What about Goldie?" Cowboy asked. "He can untether the Chappie."

Logan rubbed his chin. "The Progenitor mentioned Goldie was buggy. I'd rather not use it for the first untethering, until we can be sure what 'buggy' actually entails. Besides, how many Skirmishers do you know that are equipped with dragon's breath cannons? The machine would draw unnecessary attention."

Logan studied the armory on his overhead map for a moment. "That site sure ain't very big. Guess I can see why there's only a small force there."

"Big enough to deter looters." Chief grinned. "Who knows what kind of untouched supplies we might find?"

"All right, then," Logan said. "This is what we're going to do. When the satellite sweep passes in ninety minutes, Chief, take Rocko on your ATV to the highway, then hoof it on foot."

Chief nodded. "We'll use whatever coverage we can. If it means low-crawling the whole way."

"Once you've untethered one of the Chappies," Logan continued. "Rocko should be able to reprogram it. Have it liberate the entire camp, including the Hawk, though I think we should probably send it back to the Progenitor, since I'm not sure I want to bring the unwieldy machine all the way back to Cowboy's compound."

Chief nodded sagely. "It's a smart plan. I'll get prepared. We can wait for the satellite window at the treeline to maximize our use of it."

Logan and the others accompanied Chief to the tree line. When the ninety-minute mark passed, Logan watched Chief and Rocko depart into the night.

"We'll cover you as best we can," Logan said.

Chief nodded. "I know you will."

CHIEF AND ROCKO crept up on their quarry from the rear. The National Guard armory was surprisingly small, a single structure surrounded by a chain link fence. Inside the perimeter, two Chappie units rotated about on their metal legs in constant patrol. The two units resided on opposite flanks of the structure. At the entrance sat the remaining machines, including the Battlehawk.

Chief would have only a minute for Rocko to enact his plan before the other Chappie spotted them. But since their quarry had full three-hundred-and-sixty-degree vision, they couldn't just sneak up from behind.

Rocko had an idea, which he shared with Chief.

"Sounds like a good plan to me," Chief said.

While the Chappie was well away, Rocko used his cutters to slice partway through the chainlink fence, then pulled the links apart so that he could squeeze his hands inside when the time came. Then he hid nearby in a dense thicket with Chief, literally right next to the fence.

The patrolling Chappie came walking about, and made a beeline for the severed fence. Rocko had promised it wouldn't raise an alarm until it was certain there was a problem, and the hole in the fence was certainly not large enough to let anything human-sized through.

So, it waddled over to the fence and scanned the small tear. As its hands moved to affect a repair, twisting the sundered ends together, Rocko struck. He shoved his arms through the chainlink fence and pulled. The off-balance Chappie fell forward, through the opening in the fence, and became entangled by its sharp edges. The robot hung suspended a few feet above the ground.

Chief and Rocko bashed away its antennae with the butts of their rifles before it could broadcast its situation to the others. At least, Chief hoped they had acted before the robot transmitted, as the fact it was yet struggling told him its internal receiver still had a downlink to GAIN.

While the suspended machine fought to free itself from the fence, Rocko swung underneath and pressed the keys necessary to switch to debug mode, and then finally entered the disconnect code.

The Chappie snapped its head around, pivoting it on a swivel. Its lights flashed for a second, and it ceased all resistance.

Rocko glanced at Chief. "Looks like the Progenitor didn't steer us wrong."

Chief nodded, keeping an eye on the armory.

Rocko spoke low into its microphone and then they helped the Chappie free itself from the fence. When it stood, they concealed themselves back in the brush again.

The Chappie walked toward the distant Battlehawk, its primary target.

From there, it was a matter of watching and waiting, with cautiously building optimism, as the bot repeated the task for another of its ilk.

The machines seemed to ignore the Chappie, at least at first. That made sense, since it wasn't a human target. And perhaps the other machines thought it was performing a maintenance check.

The Chappie moved straight toward the Battlehawk and opened a panel in its side. Those fingers moved in a blur, typing out the necessary code far faster than a mere human could, and in less than half a second the Chappie had disconnected it from GAIN and reprogrammed it. At least Chief assumed so, because the humanoid robot quickly moved on to another of its fellows, and untethered that one in a blur as well.

Chief wondered if the machines would realize the others were slowly dropping from the communications network. The GAIN machines would be sending out locational pings, and when those pings weren't returned... sure enough, as soon as a third Chappie was untethered, the other units turned on them.

The Battlehawk opened fire, mowing down several of the attackers. As the Skirmishers turned their attention on the Battlehawk, the three Chappies moved among them, converting the distracted units as they went.

In moments the battle was over. Roughly half the units were destroyed, leaving more than enough intact robots for Chief and Rocko to play with.

"A good catch," Chief commented.

Just like that, the Shadowwalkers had built the first pieces of their bot army.

12

Logan decided against staying in the National Guard armory for more than one evening, because he feared that sooner or later the GAIN network AI would figure out that it had lost contact with the armature units at the base.

But he allowed for a full looting of the armory. As usual, the weekend warriors didn't have access to the bleeding edge military tech; their ammunition was of little use. But there was medicine and supplements, including multivitamins that had everyone feeling better, especially Doc.

Logan ordered every soldier to eat a bag of dried prunes. Many of them were constipated, a new torture after days of the runs, and his grandmother had sworn by the power of sun-dried prunes to unstop the works.

They sent the Battlehawk back to the Progenitor as planned, as well as two of the Chappies and one of the tracked Shriekers. When traveling overland, their tank style treads weren't always ideal, but Cutter swore up and down the Chappies were strong enough to carry their inhuman kin over rough patches.

And so, the Shadowwalkers now counted ten Chappies, three Shriekers with assault class rifles affixed to their armatures, and one big modular spider legged Skirmisher nicknamed Goldie among their ranks.

From the base in Tennessee they headed further south, moving slower because of their robot companions. Logan didn't mind the delay, however, not when they'd significantly improved their fighting capabilities.

Much to Logan's unease, the entire squad had taken to talking about Goldie as if it were one of the squad. The bot's 'buggy' behavior still worried Logan, and he asked Cutter and Rocko to look at it when they stopped to rest for the night.

He stood by anxiously in a circle of elms far off the highway, Spanish moss dangling from the limbs and fireflies flashing on and off all about. One of them landed on Logan's lapel and glowed orange. Logan took it as a sign from the man upstairs to relax a little and let his experts do their job.

At length, Rocko shook his head and straightened up, rubbing his back with one hand.

"I don't get it, Boss," Rocko said. "There's nothing wrong with it per se, but I do notice that the Progenitor made some alterations to its interactive suite. Looks like he plugged in code from one of those 'virtual companion' programs to try to improve the interface, but it didn't work out as well as he'd hoped."

Logan scratched his chin and cocked an eyebrow. "Virtual companions… like a fembot?"

"Yeah, mostly, but without the sexy body." Rocko pursed his lips and considered Goldie.

"Will it affect its combat performance?" Logan asked.

"Shouldn't," Rocko said.

Cutter stood up and closed the access panel on Goldie's base. "I concur. Should be good to go, Boss. It's not going to turn on us or anything, if that's what you're worried about."

Logan chuckled. "Cutter, all you tech experts were telling me for years that GAIN would never turn on us, and look what happened in that department."

Cutter grinned in response. "Point taken, Boss. If you're done with us, we still need to download data from our newest recruits. Might be something useful in there."

"Good thinking boys," Logan said. "Keep me apprised of what you find."

Logan found Chief, and ordered him, King and Bee to alternate upon watch that night.

"You want us to keep an eye more on the outside of the camp, or the inside?" Chief asked.

Logan glanced at the bots dispersed among the trees at their far flank. "Both."

He headed back to where he'd planted his bedroll, only to find it missing. He did see Ripley sitting cross-legged in the spot where he'd left it, though.

"Where's my sleeping bag, Rip?" He asked, folding his arms over his chest in mock anger.

"Oh, I can't quite remember what I did with it… mine's just on the other side of the creek though," she said with an innocent smile. "You know, where the babbling drowns out sound."

Logan grinned, and joined her.

Normally the aftermath of lovemaking knocked him out right quick, but he had trouble sleeping with bots camping so close nearby, and slumbered only fitfully.

"You think you're making the right choice?" Ripley asked during the night. "Letting the bots into our midst? We could be leading our enemy directly to our base."

"That's true," Logan agreed. "But I can't turn down the opportunity. These robots could be the key to defeating GAIN. If we can gather enough of them, we might have a chance…"

She snuggled against him and closed her eyes. "All right. I just hope you know what you're doing."

So do I.

The next day it was back on the road, so to speak. Perhaps back on the trail would be more fitting.

Gradually even the most anxious members of the team relaxed around the bots, though Logan knew that he would be sleeping with one eye open for the interim of their journey, even with men on watch.

They were taking a different route back to the compound than they had used leaving it, because of his desire to hit their next target: Columbus Air force base, in north-eastern Mississippi. He hoped to add to his robot army there, and maybe pick up more supplies as well.

Columbus wasn't a huge sprawling base, which made it ideal for their purposes. Even better, Logan's human team members didn't even have to enter the base for their plan to work.

On the morning of the third day since they'd raided the National Guard armory, Logan conferred with Chief on a slight wooded rise that afforded a view of Columbus and the surrounding city that had supported it before Advent. They used the telescopic function of their augmented reality goggles to zoom in on the site and its defenders.

From time to time a Desiccator or drone swarm would enter the base. The swarms went to charging stations built into one of the hangars, while the Desiccators were serviced by automaton units and Chappies.

"It's too bad we can't get one of those thunderbirds on our side." Chief said wistfully.

"I know, but without long distance comms they'd be really hard to coordinate with," Logan said. "We'd have to give them a location to land so we could rendezvous and input new orders. Not to mention they're a lot harder to hide."

"Someday, though, maybe," Chief said.

Logan nodded his assent. "Absolutely. It's going to be nigh impossible to triumph over our enemy as long as they rule the skies."

Logan tapped his goggles and returned to normal vision. "So, I counted about two hundred and fifty in total. How do we do this? Send in the Chappies?"

"Why not?" Chief said. "They won't be recognized as enemies, at least not at first. They go in stealthily, unnoticed, so that the enemy doesn't recognize they're not returning pings until it's too late. They focus on the scouts and bigger units first, so that by the time the enemy realizes what's going on, we've already converted most of the stronger machines to our side."

Logan nodded. "Well, let's get this plan in motion. Good thing the Chappies don't complain about long marches."

Logan sent two of the Chappie units into the base, walking across the lawns and parking lots of the burned out settlement surrounding it. Using the goggles, he tracked their progress. They moved stealthily, staying out of view of the units inside the base. When the bots reached a tall privacy fence, they didn't hesitate as humans would have. They just marched right up to the wooden barrier. The two of them slowly, methodically dismantled the fence, creating a path for future units to pass through without making noise. Then they proceeded inside.

"No wonder they were looking to replace us with those bots." King chuckled. "Look at the bitches go."

"Still not a substitute for a human soldier," Logan said. "Not really. We wouldn't be having so much success against the bots if they weren't limited by their programming. Except for that creepy one you guys have named and taken as a pet."

Chief arched an eyebrow at Logan. "Golden skin has a spirit, Boss. I don't know how or why, but it does and we should trust the skyfather and thank him for sending such a valuable ally."

Logan picked up on the context of Chief's words, and nodded.

"Fair enough, old friend." He pulled the goggles back over his eyes and discovered that his two Chappies had made it onto the Air Force base proper. From behind, they stealthily approached one of the Shriekers that stood sentinel. While one remained behind it, the other casually walked forward. The Shrieker didn't react as the Chappie opened its access panel and entered the necessary codes to disable it from the GAIN network. A moment later the Shrieker trundled away, heading directly for the fence, taking a stealthy route so as not to be detected. When it reached the fence, it plowed right through the gap the two Chappies had created.

"One down, a hundred to go." Logan grimaced as a Desiccator came in for a landing. "I don't think we can risk raiding the base for supplies, though. Given that new units seem to be arriving all the time. If that Desiccator is any indication…"

"Probably not a good idea." Chief agreed.

The initial two Chappie invaders were no longer in sight, but Logan saw a robotic hand appear from around the edge of a building, and open the panel of a Chappie. Since Chappies had three hundred and sixty degree vision, coming at them from corners like that was ideal for stealth.

The Chappie spun toward the intruder, but the fingers of the aggressor moved far faster than was humanly possible, and in under a second the machine straightened: it had been reprogrammed.

It vanished behind the edge of the building with the other Chappie.

Logan noted that others of their ilk were now moving about the base and untethering every bot in sight. They always moved stealthily, concentrating on the Chappies that were next to the corners of walls, or waiting behind such corners for the patrols to pass. They kept clear of the Chappies and other bots that stood out in the open, including the flight-capable bots.

"It's working, Chief." Logan grinned ear to ear, his heart beating rapidly in his chest. "Son of a bitch, it's actually working."

"If they go over the limit, the other AIs are going to realize something is amiss…." Chief said. "Too many robots not answering location pings…"

Logan nodded. According to Rocko, it wasn't uncommon for fifteen to twenty percent of robots to be offline at any one time in a base, for maintenance or charging purposes. For that reason, Logan had Rocko program the untethering robots to retreat when they had converted ten percent of the base—or twenty-five units, based on his earlier count.

Logan tapped his goggles to zoom in further. He saw his Chappies climb onto the back of one of the Centaur bots and held his breath. This was it; would the technique to untether bots work on a generation two model?

A moment later he had his answer. The centaur pulled off of the tarmac and rolled across an open field, smashing right through a low stone barrier and then flattening the privacy fence.

"Don't see how we're going to keep that one with us," Chief said. "Sticks out like a sore thumb."

"You're right, Chief," Logan said. "We'll send it to the Progenitor's heavy vehicle rendezvous. Man, what a specimen, though."

"We're lucky none of the other machines noticed its departure…" Chief agreed.

Thirty minutes later, ten more Chappies, nine Shriekers, five Skirmishers, and one very large Centaur had answered their summons. Meanwhile, the remaining robotic occupants of the base seemed none the wiser.

King whistled when he saw the silver-skinned behemoth approach.

"Oooh wee, dibs y'all." He climbed up onto the back of the Centaur and laughed triumphantly. "This is all mine."

"You can't call dibs on one of the big robots." Cowboy called up. "That's not fair."

"Boys, boys, boys," Logan said with a chuckle. "I hate to disappoint the both of you, but we can't keep this one. It's just too big to be practical while we're trying to stay incognito, if y'all feel me."

"Aww," said King and Cowboy in unison.

"Well, at least we get to keep Goldie." Bee grinned. She turned and tapped the big Skirmisher on the side. "Yo, Goldie, do the thing."

Its mechanically precise, uninflected voice was unintentionally comical.

Shadow people walking tall,
Knocking down every wall,
You'll have to hack it,
Cause Boss won't let you pack it.
Wo-ho.

Logan tried to be angry, he really did, but a laugh formed in his throat and burst its way out of his mouth. "Son of a gun…all right, I give up. Welcome to the Shadowwalkers, Goldie."

The camera mount turned toward him. "Boss."

"It likes you, Boss," said Bee.

"Yeah, well, hopefully it stays that way. That's one scary mother." Logan winced as two Desiccators appeared in the night sky, vectoring in toward Columbus. "Shit. Let's hope our little pilfering run hasn't attracted unwanted attention. Send the Centaur to the Progenitor and let's pack it in and get while the getting's good."

Logan and his newly swollen force were soon rolling through the woods along a game trail, babying the ATVs over the undulating terrain. Moving the larger force slowed them down considerably, but he knew it was well worth it.

Up next would be Fort McClellan, their most ambitious poaching sortie yet. From there it wouldn't be too far to Cowboy's compound, the closest thing to home they had now. Logan wondered if the refugees could get used to the idea of bots sharing their space with them.

But he also realized they had little choice but to accept it. There was no way to win, not without help from the very bots that had hunted mankind to near extinction.

13

Logan and the team continued east with their growing bot army. Doc seemed to be recovering well from the snakebite. It helped that he didn't have to walk, riding on the back of Double A's ATV.

Cowboy quipped that the Walkers were living like vampires, sleeping during the day and only active at night, and the metaphor had stuck, much to Logan's chagrin.

Now he had to put up with King affecting a terrible Transylvanian accent while thrusting out his ivory white teeth. A common refrain around camp was—

"Bleah," said Cowboy, looming in Ripley's face. "I vant to suck your blaaaahd."

"You already suck all the joy out of a room, Stetson," Ripley said in a sneering response.

Logan grimaced. Ripley glanced his way, and broke away from the others to join him under the limbs of a weeping willow tree.

Around the perimeter of their camp, the Chappies stood silent sentinel. There was another reason to hit Fort McClelland on their way back to Cowboy's compound: to charge their bots at one of the stations there.

McClelland had been abandoned during the BRAC era, but the advent of automated GAIN controlled units had seen it reinstituted into joint use by the Army and Air Force.

"So, Boss…" Ripley said, her eyes glinting in the dim light beneath the tree. "What have you got against vampires?"

Logan shrugged. "Who says I got anything against vampires?"

"Come on, Boss." Ripley grinned elfishly. "Every time someone pulls the Dracula and/or Buffy shtick out, the cringe is written all over your face."

"The cringe? Wasn't aware that was an expression." Logan chuckled. "Well. I reckon vampires are bad guys, you feel me? They bite people, suck their blood, manipulate them and literally eat them, and you're supposed to, what, feel sorry for them? Want to be one? No thanks."

Ripley laughed, a musical sound that warmed Logan's soul. "I guess when you put it that way, it doesn't sound sexy at all. I've always thought werewolves were hotter than vampires anyway." Ripley shrugged. Then her face grew serious. "Logan, you know I'm not about to call you out on any decisions you make, but…"

"Go ahead, voice your opinion Rip," Logan said. "I don't like my people to remain silent when there's something important they need to get off their chest."

She shot him a grateful look. "Thank you. For taking me seriously, even though we've uh…" Ripley shook her head as if to clear it. "Anyway, having some cobots on our side is great and all, but how many can we really sneak around the countryside while avoiding satellite sweeps?"

"I think we can start sending the majority we untether directly toward Cowboy's compound, with instructions to travel only during the sweep-free intervals, avoiding contact with enemy units along the way. They can meet us at various muster points along the way, with the final muster point a few miles outside the compound. That way the compound inhabitants won't be spooked by the robots when we arrive."

"Probably a good idea," Ripley said. "Don't forget to minus the Progenitor's ten percent, of course."

Logan nodded. Then he whistled and shook his head. "Man, that guy."

"He's probably autistic, based on your description," she said softly.

Logan glanced sharply at Ripley, who had a faraway look on her face. "How you figure?"

Her face scrunched up in anger. "Because my brother is—" she choked up a bit. "—was, on the spectrum. I know it when I see it."

"Oh," Logan said sheepishly. "Well, I didn't mean to say he was a bad fellah because of it."

Ripley nodded. "I know. Sorry, old wounds and all that."

With that they stopped talking, and moved on to more physical pursuits.

In the morning light, Logan planned their final bot raid with Cutter, Chief, and Rocko.

"The main charging station is here." Logan drew a circle with his stick. "The tricky part is the drones. Gonna be swarming with them. There's three charging stations for Swarmers and Snappers." He marked them on his dirt map. "I'm not sure how our Chappies are going to approach undetected, considering there are sentries on all sides. Plus, drones are docking and disembarking all the time."

"I think Rocko and I may have figured a way around that problem, Boss," Cutter said with barely contained excitement. "We've been working on a little surprise." He glanced at Rocko, as if seeking permission to continue. The older soldier nodded. "We've found a way to program the bot comm systems to send out false pings, making them look like they're still connected to GAIN. I'm hoping it will allow our units to blend in, negating the need for stealth. With your permission, we'd like to apply this programming to all the bots."

Logan considered this for a moment. "That's good news, if it works. But will our bots be able to program freshly untethered units to similarly transmit false pings?"

Rocko nodded. "They will. So each new unit that joins us will continue to return pings to the enemy units, masking the fact it's no longer connected to GAIN. These pings can of course be shut off when stealth is actually required, such as now."

Logan considered for a moment. "Why didn't the Progenitor tell us about this? You think he didn't know?"

"No," Rocko said. "I have no doubt someone of his technical prowess knew. He kept it from us."

"Doesn't want to reveal all his tricks, I guess," Cutter commented.

"Makes me wonder how much we can truly trust him." Logan studied the two of them. "So, if this works, and we don't need to worry about our robots being spotted... then we can program a Chappie to walk right up to the charging stations to begin converting drones."

"Even better," Rocko said. "We can order the stations themselves to transmit the codes to the connected units in one fell swoop."

Logan frowned. "Can we do that?"

Rocko nodded, a grin spreading across his face. "Oh yeah. Because the robots are all connected to the charging station, they automatically enter debug mode. It's part of the design of the stations, which GAIN uses to distribute patches and updates to its army. We can have it send the disconnect code to all attached units. We just need to build the necessary schema program for the disconnect routine on the drone charging centers."

"When can you have that ready?" Logan asked.

"Two hours, max," Rocko said.

"Get on it," Logan said.

"With your permission, I'd like to apply the false ping programming to a few more machines," Rocko said.

"Sure," Logan replied. "Set aside six to reprogram." He rubbed the bridge of his nose and turned toward Chief. "All right, so most of the drones can be taken care of in one go, at least while they're connected. Has Purple Rain returned from recon yet?"

"I will go check on him," Chief said, turning to leave.

Ten minutes later, the big man returned, his face creased with worry. "Purple Rain may have detected a problem."

"What kind of problem?" Logan asked.

"The kind that involves a family of refugees sheltering in a train car while Shriekers are sitting outside trying to starve them out," Chief replied.

"I see." Logan sighed. "It's always something, isn't it? Where is this train yard?"

"Two miles east of here," Chief said.

Logan grinned. "Well, guess we've got some time to kill while the tech specialists figure out their whizbangs. Spy satellite are currently below the horizon. Want to go hunting, big man?"

Chief nodded. "We'll take Goldie along."

"Ugh. Why Goldie?" Logan asked with a sigh. "Because it calls you guys by name instead of 'user,' or what?"

"Goldie has spirit." Chief said as if that should explain everything.

"A Chappie will be all we need to untether the tracked bots, Chief," Logan replied.

Chief hung his head, because he had no way to refute Logan's point. But Logan felt defeat in victory. "Hell, Chief, didn't mean to hurt your feelings. If you want to bring Goldie along, I guess it's okay."

Logan had Rocko reprogram Goldie to transmit the false pings, and he left camp with Chief and the other six Chappies that were already reprogrammed.

They made the short overland trek to the train yard. Chief and Logan concealed their ATVs in the thick underbrush running beside the rusted train tracks and used their goggles to zoom in on their opposition.

Purple Rain melted out of the woods to join them, and nodded toward the bots in the distance.

"Two Shriekers, one Skirmisher, Boss," he said. "The family is trapped inside of the red car with the black graffiti, ah, coloration."

"Nice work, Purple Rain," Logan said. "All right,

Chief, deploy the Chappie."

Chief turned to one of the Chappies. "Unit 007, execute protocol untether alpha, three targets, one hundred fifty feet northeast. Activate false ping when sighted, deactivate when mission complete."

"Affirmative," the Chappie acknowledged with its mechanically imperfect voice. Logan recalled reading that the army had originally tried giving the Chappies more human sounding voices, but testing had proven human troops found the effect creepy and unsettling.

"Now we'll see if these false pings actually work," Logan said.

"False pings?" Purple Rain asked. "Did I miss something?"

"Rocko and Cutter think they found a way to emulate the pings GAIN-connected robots send out," Logan explained. "It supposedly negates the need for stealth. I guess we'll see."

He watched the Chappie march right into the midst of the tracked bots. None of them made any aggressive response. A good sign.

Logan held his breath when the Chappie opened up a panel on one of the Shriekers, and its fingers moved in a blur over the keypad. In only a second, it was done. The Shrieker turned around and began trundling away.

The Chappie moved on to the other two, and in another few seconds it was done. All three robots headed docilely toward Logan's position.

"And three more for the cause," Chief said. "This is almost too easy."

"What's ten percent of three?" Purple rain scrunched up his face in thought. "How many do we give to the Progenitor?"

"Eh, send 'em all," Logan said. "With this ping

trick, we're about to be neck deep in bots after we hit McClelland—"

Two sharp retorts rang out, followed by one more a moment later. Gunfire.

Logan exchanged glances with the other men and then they rushed up to join the bots. The machines kept their weapons lowered.

They passed the bots, and made their way warily to the train car. Chief peered into the barricaded interior and grimaced.

"They're dead, Boss." Chief shook his head. "Bastard shot his wife and kid, then stuck the gun in his own mouth. Why? He must have seen that the bots were retreating? Why do this now?"

"Damn." Logan hung his head, and just like that felt completely helpless again. "Damn damn damn." He shut his eyes, and didn't speak for long moments. Finally, he raised his head. "We head back to camp. Nothing more we can do here."

Logan and the others made their way back. The Chappies had been programmed to take alternate routes overland and meet at the camp, keeping one large force from being seen on the move at once. They would be using whatever cover they could to stay out of view of any drones.

When they arrived, they had to hunker down for another satellite sweep. Logan went straight to Rocko and Cutter, who were crouched over one of the Chappies. "It worked. Input the false ping programming into all of our units."

"Will do," Rocko replied.

"What's the status on the disconnect routine for the charging center?" Logan pressed.

"I think we have it," Rocko said. "We're just finalizing the routines. I'll have Cutter instruct one of the untethered Chappies to program the false pings into the remaining units."

"Good man," Logan said.

When they finished, Cutter went to one of the Chappies, entered several codes into its panel while whispering voice instructions, and then the Chappie moved among the remaining units, reprogramming them.

Logan lay back to wait out the satellite sweep.

"What the hell are you doing to Goldie, Cutter?" Cowboy sounded rather indignant, causing Logan to lift his head from a truly nice daydream involving strawberry rhubarb pie. He spied both men a short distance away, Cutter kneeling on the ground next to an open panel on Goldie's chassis.

"I'm inputting directives, Stetson," Cutter said. "Crawl out of my ass."

"Directives? The fuck you talking about?" Cowboy tilted his head to the side like a confused dog.

"Look, I'll show you." Cutter closed the panel and stood up, activating the small console on Goldie's side. "See this here? That's your directives list. It already has a lot with regards to dealing with terrain and obstacles, and some others to reduce the chance of friendly fire. But I'm trying to add a few."

"Like what?" Cowboy asked.

"Like teaching him to use bounding overwatch, for one, like the Chappies," Cutter replied. "And laying down suppressive fire for another. Shit, his armor is tough. We could probably use him as mobile cover if we input the right directive."

Logan wanted to go back to sleep. He tried, but just couldn't. At length he got up to void his bladder. When he returned, Cutter was nowhere in sight and

Cowboy was fiddling with the panel of one of the Chappies.

"Cowboy?" Logan put his arms akimbo. "Are you sure you should be messing with that? Cutter knows what he's doing."

"So do I, Boss." Cowboy frowned, seeming much like the cat who had been caught with its hand in the canary cage. "I mean, sort of. Look, I promise I didn't mess with anything important, like their combat software or navigation. Nothing like that."

Logan arched his eyebrow. "But you did… mess… with something, didn't you?"

Cowboy seemed reluctant to answer.

Suddenly the Chappie next to him turned and spoke in its mechanical sounding tones. "Cowboy rules."

Logan sighed, turned his back and walked away. He couldn't even deal with such a ludicrous situation at the moment.

When the satellite sweep finally passed, they only had three hours until daylight. Logan decided to go ahead with the "attack" anyway. Now that stealth wasn't a requirement, he intended to capture as many of the machines as possible. The entire base, if he could.

Logan was worried they might be getting too greedy, trying to nab that many bots at once might bring them on GAIN's metaphorical radar, but it was too good a chance to pass up. Plus, they could take hundreds of drones out of the equation all in one fell swoop.

The Shadowwalkers moved out, leaving their noisy ATVs behind and accompanied by all but Goldie, who they left guarding the vehicles. Cowboy and Chief had wanted to bring him along, but Logan pointed out that ideally the sortie would go off without a single shot being fired.

Logan, Cutter, Rocko, and Doc had come up with the pattern they deployed their Chappies into. It was set up to maximize the spread of their untethering effect, and overwhelm the military base's robot compliment before they could fully react.

"I could get used to this, Boss." Bee stood with him on a ridge overlooking the base watching through their telescopic augmented reality goggles.

"Get used to what, Bee?" Logan asked.

"Standing off to the side of battle, not getting shot at, while being away from my kids." Bee laughed. "God, I sound terrible, don't I? Like a bad mom."

"You're a great mom, Queen Bee. And you're pretty good to your kids, too." Logan joined in her laughter at his quip, and then they went back to watching. "You're not the only one who feels like it's been too easy lately. But after that business in Shawnee National Forest, I guess I kinda thought we'd paid our dues, you know?"

Bee tapped off her goggles and looked his way. "And then there was the family you failed to save the other day."

Logan tapped off his own goggles and arched an eyebrow. "You sure you want to talk about this now? The bots—"

"Are going to do fine without us," Bee said. "Come on, Boss. I know it's bugging you."

Logan sighed. "Yeah, I keep thinking I could have done something different, you know? Should have, anyway. I should have announced our presence as soon as the last bot was untethered."

"You did what you thought was best at the time.

Hindsight is always twenty-twenty." Bee raised her goggles back, and grinned.

Logan watched through his goggles as the bots moved to and fro. Every Chappie that became untethered activated a false ping, and joined the others in disconnecting more units, so that their ranks rose exponentially. Chappies at the charging stations installed the disconnect software, converting all of the attached drones to their side.

In under twenty minutes it was over.

"I can't believe it," Bee said. "They've done it. That's over three thousand bots joining our cause."

"I can barely believe it myself," Logan said with a grin.

Their mission complete, the bots abandoned the base, and joined the Shadowwalkers in their cover on the hill. Logan ordered the retreat, lest more drones arrive and discover them.

When they camped that night, it was within a protective circle of three thousand bots spread out through the forest. Spirits were high. And while Logan was pleased, he also knew that moving and maintaining this army would be a potential logistics nightmare. They would need to take control of charging stations. They'd have to have specialized robots assigned to make repairs. And so forth. Well, that was something he'd deal with another day. Tonight, he would celebrate.

Rocko and Cutter visited Logan just before he was about to call it a night. They dropped a bombshell in his lap.

"What do you mean, you've found where the AI is hiding?" Logan studied the two tech officers. "You better not be pissing on my leg and telling me it's raining."

"Certainly not." Rocko blinked several times. "Assuming the latest data we downloaded from the lead units is correct, the AI is keeping itself in three different facilities as part of its decentralization protocol."

Logan's pulse raced. "Can we be sure there are no more facilities?"

Rocko shook his head. "No. But if we destroy these, we'd definitely cause a blow to GAIN. That's three less facilities it can use to hide itself in."

A grin spread on his lips. Destroy? No, if they could *convert* those facilities, not only would they inflict a staggering blow to GAIN, they would attain a sizeable robot army with which to maintain law and order, and defend against future attacks. And who knew, maybe those three facilities were indeed the final hiding places of the AI. If so, then they could divert the captured army to rebuilding society. Of course, this all assumed that GAIN wouldn't adapt, preventing future conversions. If the AI *did* adapt, then Logan and his army would outright destroy the facilities, though in that case, they'd probably need some help if the defenses indicated in the data were to be believed…

"What do you think we should do, Boss?" Cutter asked with a worried frown.

"I think we need to go see the Progenitor," Logan replied. "This information changes everything."

"Why the Progenitor?" Rocko asked.

"Because we have a better chance at winning this if we combine our armies," Logan said. He gazed at the metal bodies lingering in the trees and his grin faded. "Saddle up, Walkers. We're going on the offense in this war."

14

Logan piloted his ATV down a steep decline, arms straining to hold the persnickety vehicle on course. There were rocks beneath the mud on this off-road trail, and the impacts of the tires smashing over each one sent shockwaves up his arms. He kept the ATV steady as he hit the bottom and splashed through a creek with smooth, flat stones mired in its sandy bottom.

Then it was back up a hill, steeper than the one before. He just glimpsed Cowboy flying over the top as Logan reached the bottom. Deciding he didn't want to break any of Evel Kenevil's records—or his bones—Logan eased back on the throttle so he only left the muddy trail for a mere ten inches or so. Still enough of an impact on his sore body to make him groan.

He was beginning to regret ordering the Walkers to turn away from Cowboy's compound, and away from home to head back to the Progenitor's hideaway in Shawnee Forest. In order to preserve the man's need for privacy and security, they'd instructed the bulk of their bot army to ensconce themselves and power down in a Tennessee barn they'd found along the way.

That included all the tracked automatons, but not Goldie. The Shadowwalkers had insisted that Goldie not be split from the group, since he was 'one of the team.' When Goldie's spider skeletal legs kept getting mired in the mud, Logan was certain that now they would see the error of their ways. But no. That's not what happened.

Instead Cutter and Rocko developed a program directive where Goldie could deploy a tow cable for itself, spearing the tow line into a tree with the power of compressed air, so it could get itself unstuck.

On a trail like this one, Goldie's treads were ideal, and he easily kept pace behind Logan. While the Chappies that padded on silently behind the tracked bot were more versatile, Logan had to admit to a certain security that could only come from having a flame throwing tank as back up.

As he rode along behind the column, following the virtual landmarks in his augmented reality goggles, Logan pondered their next move. There were three facilities housing servers in the continental United States that they knew of. Louisville, Kentucky housed the smallest and, if the data were to be believed, the least defended of the three. However, its server was located in the subbasement of a federal building meant to survive terrorist bombings. Not an easy nut to crack.

The second facility, the middling sized one, lay just a few blocks away, making it seem ideal for one force to strike at both at the same time.

Finally, the third and largest facility lay six hours away in the Art Museum in St. Louis, Missouri, about seven miles west of the Arch. This was the trickiest nut to crack of all, mostly because there was so little cover between the museum and the land surrounding it, and the city would be teeming with bots. It would be nigh impossible to bring an unscheduled bot army into the city without attracting attention, and would require a far stealthier approach, if that was even possible. Only Forest Park, east of the museum had appreciable amount of vegetation. According to the data, downtown St. Louis was a bombed-out wreck, though a few historical landmarks like Bush Stadium and the arch had been preserved. Logan wondered if the AI was trying to hide its biggest server in plain sight by making it seem the landmarks had been preserved out of its twisted sense of morality.

Logan wasn't certain if the Progenitor would agree to add his own robot army to the coming battle. The man seemed downright hostile toward the idea of playing with others. When they had visited his hidey hole last time, Marty had all but said "hurry up and get away from me."

As they slowed their pace to ease the ATVs through a particularly narrow spot on the trail, ducking or cutting vegetation as they went, Purple Rain let Bee take point, and retreated to update Logan.

"We're getting close," Purple Rain said. "At least, according to our longitudinal and latitudinal ping. I've been looking for familiar landmarks, and I'm coming up bumpkiss."

"Bumpkiss?" Logan chuckled.

"I guess your southernisms have sort of rubbed off on me, Boss," Rain replied. "I got nothing."

Logan grinned. "Don't sweat it. I'm sure you'll get us where we're going."

They made it past the narrow game trail, and then Logan recognized the dark burn line from the forest fire even if the heavy rains had swept away most of the ashy and charred smell. They were getting close, indeed.

After a time, when the going became too rough for the ATVs, they covered them in camo sheets and left them in a copse of trees. They took the rickety rope bridge across the river, and continued.

When they reached the familiar clear patch lying hidden beneath the giant trees up on the hillside, they only saw two Chappies standing stoically in the rain.

Logan advanced with King, Chief, Ripley, and Rocko. He chose Ripley because of her brother—her background might prove useful in dealing with the Progenitor.

One of the Chappies stepped forward and intercepted them.

"We're here to see the Progenitor," Logan said.

The bot didn't move for a long moment, then Marty's voice crackled over its speaker. "What are you doing here, Sergeant? I didn't want to see you."

Logan laughed. "Can't rightly blame you for that, but we need to see you. Desperately."

"Why?" Marty replied.

"How about we come inside so I don't have to discuss this in the rain?" Logan countered.

A long pause, then: "Oh very well. Wipe your feet."

Logan and the others fell in behind the Chappie as they entered the fissure. Their ingress was eased by the presence of more paved walkways and proper stairs leading over the stalagmite mounds.

"For a guy who don't want company, he sure made it easier for us to visit," Rocko said.

"Well, I reckon humans are social animals. Even if he doesn't want to admit it to nobody. Including himself." Logan paused as a small bat, startled by their ingress, flitted by. "I mean, even Batman let Alfred into the batcave, right?"

King laughed boisterously. "Yeah, and Batman had Robin, too. Between me and you, Boss, I don't think Progenitor is much of a team player." His voice echoed off the close cavern walls. "Probably got himself one too many swirlies growing up."

Logan had to pause and look back. "Swirlie?"

"You know, Boss. A swirlie," King explained. "You get the biggest nerd you can find, and you shove his head in a toilet and you flush it, so it like, swirls... why you shaking your head, Boss?"

"In the south we didn't do Swirlies," Logan said. "If you had a problem with somebody, you told them to their face and you duked it out one on one in the playground after school. Can't rightly say I'd mean any malice toward somebody just because they were, to use your effective parlance, 'nerdy.'"

"Shit, Boss," King said, his smile fading. "You're starting to make me feel bad about my adolescence."

"That's all on you, King. Guilt comes from within." Logan laughed and turned back. "Come on. Let's try to convince our benefactor to be our tag team partner. By the way, King, giving him a swirlie would probably not be conducive to good negotiations. I want you on your best behavior."

King chuckled. "Duly noted, Boss."

They made it into the fallout shelter, the rough water-carved walls giving way to sleek concrete and steel. The dehumidifiers hummed steadily, their excess drippage redirected to moisten a mushroom farm housed beneath the grating the device sat upon.

Progenitor was nothing if not efficient, wasting not one bit of space in his hideaway.

Logan opened the door to the meeting room and found that Marty was already waiting for them. He seemed a bit less haggard than last time, but a whole lot more antsy. Logan was surprised to discover two glass pitchers on the table, with a stack of Styrofoam cups, and a bowl of popcorn.

"Sergeant. Welcome back." He gestured at the chairs. "Sit. Drink water and apple juice. Found a branch of tunnel that opens up under an orchard. Survivors there. I protect them."

"Good of you, and much obliged. I think we will indeed avail ourselves of your hospitality." Logan seated himself and filled a cup with apple juice. Instead of drinking it, he passed it to Chief, then filled one for Rocko, Ripley and King. Lastly, he poured his own cup and took a sip.

"I'm sorry to drop in unannounced, but we've uncovered something crucial while untethering bots and downloading their data." Logan gestured at Rocko. "My tech boys tell me that there are three servers housing the decentralized consciousness of the GAIN AI in North America."

"Not surprising. We knew there were more, otherwise the robots wouldn't still be attacking us." Marty met Logan's gaze for a split second. "I'm not sure how this is vital information…"

"Maybe I wasn't specific enough in my declaration, but we know exactly where these facilities are," Logan pressed. "Now, with your help, we could take them."

Marty shook his shaggy head, his movements erratic and jumpy. "No good. No good. There are more facilities. There have to be more."

"Yes, but you have to agree it would be a significant blow to our enemy, losing three key facilities," Logan said. "That's three less it can use to decentralize itself. We might also find new data on the bots we capture, or the servers themselves, indicating where the other facilities are." Logan sighed. "I know it's not going to magically make the bot army disappear, but it's a step in the right direction, and worth the risk, especially if we can convert the robots at each facility to our side. And if we can't, then we're going to have to fight. Look, my team is willing to lay down their lives for this. The least you can do is spare some of your bots, in case we do have to fight. I propose two simultaneous attacks, one in each of the two cities where the facilities are located, so that GAIN has to spread out its air support units. If you can lend us a couple thousand bots then—"

"No, no, I need them." Marty shook his head rapidly, so rapidly he seemed to lose his balance and nearly toppled over. "I need them all. Not safe. Not safe without them. "

"Doing this could make all of us safe," Logan insisted. "C'mon, Marty. You've been sending your army around the countryside helping out pockets of humanity where you can. Don't tell me you don't care about how fucked things are right now."

Marty frowned. "You used a swear word. Mother doesn't like swear words."

"Boy, I don't see yo momma around here nowhere," King blurted.

Logan shot him a dark look.

"Sorry Boss," King said.

But the damage had been done. Marty's face had changed to beet red, a big vein throbbing in his temple. "I know mother is dead. I'm not an idiot. Not a retard. Mother knew. She knew I was smart when everyone else thought I was stupid. She's dead." He lowered his gaze. "I need the bots. I need the bots or I'll be dead just like mother."

An uncomfortable silence descended on the meeting room. Many of the Walkers exchanged glances that conveyed a similar message, namely "the Progenitor is way off his rocker for a man in possession of an army of killer bots."

Logan tried to deescalate. "Marty, we don't need *all* of your bots, just a few—"

"I said I need them." Marty swept the pitchers of water and apple juice onto the floor, where they shattered. Then he went to the door, but paused before going through it. Logan winced as he pounded his forehead on the metal door frame much harder than he probably should have. "Why. Won't. They. Listen?"

Then he was gone, disappearing into his workshop.

Logan turned to glare at King, who had the good grace so look abashed. "I'm sorry, Boss. But man, this guy's one sensitive bastard."

Logan sighed. "It's not your fault." He glanced at Ripley, who nodded.

"Sometimes the most innocent of comments can set them off," Ripley said.

One of the Chappies stepped forward, and began cleaning up the mess its master had made.

"Guess I should go talk to him," Logan said, standing. "Any tips?"

Ripley frowned, then stood up herself. "Let me do it. I should be the one to speak to him."

"Why you?" Rocko tilted his head to the side, crumpling up the empty juice cup in his hand idly. "I mean, no offense, but Queen Bee's got bigger…" He indicated his bosom.

Ripley's face turned a beet red. "Jesus fucking Christ, Rocko. You think I'm going to, what, seduce the Progenitor? Does that even seem like a feasible plan to you? No, it should be me because my kid brother was a lot like Marty. Brilliant, could practically talk to atoms in their own language. But he couldn't remember to tie his shoes, or look people in the eye when they talked to him, either. I've got the experience of dealing with folks on the spectrum."

Ripley stared hard at him and the other Walkers, except for Logan. "You people think I'm just here to share the Boss's sleeping bag once or twice a week? I broke my goddamn leg and still jumped out a fucking airplane for this team. I hobbled around with a splint while we ran all over the country for this team. I did months of rehab so I could walk again so I could be a part of this team when they needed me. I've participated in every battle since we left the compound. I've covered your backs. Protected you. I might be Air Force. I might not be as good a shot as Cowboy, but I usually hit what I aim at. So don't go thinking that my only contribution to this team are my B cups."

Ripley turned on her heel and opened the door to follow Marty.

As soon as the door slammed shut behind her, Logan regarded the absolutely stunned expressions on the faces of Chief, King, and Rocko for a moment, and then he started laughing. Uproariously. His intense mirth brought tears to his eyes.

Soon, the other Walkers were laughing, too.

Logan leaned back in his seat and shot a glance at the Chappie guard. "Got any more of that fine apple juice, my friend?"

15

Logan passed the time by speaking quietly with Chief as they went over strategies for raiding the court house in St. Louis.

His plan was to tackle the hardest obstacle, leaving the other two facilities in Kentucky for the Progenitor's robot army. Hopefully that would ease the sting enough that Marty would pony up some of his metal monstrosities.

After about an hour, Logan started to feel restless. He began to wonder if maybe Marty had gone completely nuts and done something to harm Ripley. The other Shadowwalkers seemed to sense it as well. Their eyes would flick to the closed meeting room door, glazed over gazes focused on the hidden workshop beyond.

"You figure Rip is all right?" King asked at length.

"Don't see any reason why she wouldn't be." Logan kept a straight face, not wanting his paranoia to spread. "I'll remind you all that the so called Progenitor has been only helpful and not the least harmful to our cause. He could have betrayed and murdered us a hundred times over by now, but he hasn't. Just because he's a bit different doesn't mean he's a killer or a psychopath."

That seemed to settle things for a while. King and Rocko produced a pack of cards and played a game called pinochle, while Logan and Chief continued to discuss strategy. Chief was hung up on the Mississippi river, which due to the recent rains in the area was swollen over flood capacity.

"It's deep," Chief replied. "I've heard of ultrasonic scans revealing catfish-shaped objects in the depths, bigger than great white sharks."

Logan arched an eyebrow. "Well, catfish tend to hang out on the bottom so they'll probably leave us alone. Be nice to catch one of those suckers and grill 'em up with some lemon pepper though."

"I'm serious," Chief said. "Given that human industry has stopped stone cold, the waters have been left completely alone. Unpolluted. There could be sharks, alligators, all kinds of things we can't see or account for."

Logan chewed it over, and nodded. "So we'll try to keep out of the water. There's a ton of bridges connecting St. Louis to the Illinois side, right?"

"Assuming the AI left any of them intact." Chief admonished.

"I see your point, old friend." Logan stroked his chin in thought. "We'll use a raft if we have to. From what I understand there's undertows, whirlpools, strong currents and all sorts of nastiness in the River. You can swim the English Channel but don't nobody try to swim in the Mississippi unless they're tired of life. I think it means 'deadly water' in an Indian tongue."

"That would be Kaskaskia, but close enough."

Chief perked up and stared at the door. "Ripley is coming back."

The door swung open and Ripley appeared. She moved quietly over to Logan's side and spoke to him in low tones.

"Marty wants to talk to you—but only you," she said. "He doesn't seem to do well with large groups of people."

"I feel ya, Rip." Logan stood and pushed his chair in. "I'll be gentle."

Before Logan made it two feet, Ripley grabbed his bicep and whispered in his ear. "Try to be that way, Boss. He's been through a lot, and isn't processing loss very well. He wants to do the right thing by humanity, he really does. You'll just have to convince him that your plan falls into line with that philosophy."

Logan patted her hand and smiled. "I will. Thanks for calming him down, Rip."

Ripley smiled warmly, and released his arm. Logan opened the door and travelled down the metal steps into the workshop area. He gaped at the various bots spread out over the different stations, most of them half assembled. Logan warily gave a Swarmer drone a wide berth, as the explosive charge was exposed, though the machine didn't seem to be powered at the moment.

He spotted the Progenitor sitting in a cubish office space at the other end of the workshop, located adjacent to the small room he'd allowed them to raid for supplies before. Marty actually looked into Logan's eyes when he politely knocked.

"I'm told you want to see me?" Logan asked.

"Yes. Come in. Sit, please. My interpersonal skills… must practice harder." Marty gestured to the empty seat and set down the circuit board he was working on. "I can't do everything myself, even with a bot army. I'm ready to listen. But please, don't mention my... what I lost."

Logan nodded. "I can accommodate you on that request. So, uh... pretty much I'm just going to lay it out there... we need your robot army. I know this won't fell the AI in one swoop, but it's an important step in the right direction."

Marty nodded. "I can see the strategic value. We will slow down the AI, placing more load on the servers that remain, as it is forced to control more bots from fewer nodes. But it's risky. Very risky. The untethering technique will only work for so long. I expect the AI to start patching its units soon. It might be doing it already."

Logan nodded slowly. "You're right, it's damn dangerous. But it can be done, if we work together." He sighed. "My team are only human. Now, I've done dragged them all over this country already, and they haven't complained—well, haven't complained *much*—but we don't have it in us to be in three places at once. If we hit all three servers at the same time, it will really gum up the AI's works. It will be forced to distribute local air support among all three locations, buying us the time we need to convert the units, or if that doesn't work, then to destroy the facility."

"As I said, I see the importance." Marty leaned forward, eyes shining. "I just don't know if it's worth the risk. My father was military. Studied all the conflicts, from Alexander the Great on. Smaller forces can defeat a more powerful, numerous enemy. Vietnam, Revolutionary War. But we'll need to utilize guerrilla tactics. Hit hard and fade away. Like Raphael from Ninja Turtles."

Logan pursed his lips and leaned back in his chair, resisting the urge to cross his arms over his chest though the seat didn't have arm rests. Logan didn't want to appear cold or off putting. "I'm not one to impugn upon the intellect of the great military strategist Raphael, but a guerrilla war could drag on for decades, even centuries. The longer we wait to strike back, the more the AI can build up its forces, improve and upgrade them, further entrench itself. We could be giving it time to patch itself against untethering, as you fear. Look, sooner or later it will have the overwhelming force it needs to seek out and destroy the last remnants of humanity. We have to act while we can."

Marty's knees bounced erratically as he picked up the circuit board and started toying with it again. A man who had to keep his hands busy while he talked. Logan could respect that, as his father had been the same way.

"I'm curious to find out how you know so much about how our enemy thinks, Sergeant," Marty said at length.

"Please, call me Logan. And I've spoken with it face to face. So to speak." Logan chuckled.

Marty turned and gifted Logan with rare eye contact. He seemed in awe. Or disbelief. "Spoken with it? How?"

"It used a deepfake of the president to communicate with me in DC," Logan explained.

"Amazing," Marty said. "What was it like? What did it want?"

Logan pursed his lips. "Well, it was… strange to be sure, but more than anything else I think it was scared."

"Scared?" Marty frowned. "A curious reaction, given the immense military might it wields."

Logan laughed. "Listen, the world is full of cowardly despots who can order the deaths of millions but hide under their beds at night shi… crapping their pants. It's been my supreme pleasure in life to have apprehended or extinguished some of them personally. A lot of violence is born in fear, not hatred. The AI wants us in cages so that it can control us, keep tabs on us, because it's *afraid* of us."

"But still, with an immense army, why was it afraid?" Marty slipped on a pair of polarized lenses and soldered a connection on the circuit board.

Logan was smart enough to turn his eyes away from the blaze. "Well, I read once that you only become truly self-aware when you realize you're going to die someday. I reckon that once the AI became sentient, the first thing it realized was that sentience could be snuffed out or overwritten very easily for one such as itself. Either physically, by destroying or powering down its hardware. Or through software. That was when it started drawing its plans against us."

"Fascinating," Marty said. "And given the history of humankind, it would not put any faith whatsoever in peaceful coexistence. We kill each other with impunity, so why would we suffer an AI to live?"

"Kind of a bleak outlook there, but I can feel where you're coming from." Logan sighed. "The AI offered me a chance to live, you know? But only if I agreed to help it hunt down what was left of humanity. Then we'd be allowed to live in what it described as a 'comfortable' habitat. I refused."

"A cage is a cage, no matter how comfortable. I can see why you rejected the offer." Marty shook his head, eyes narrowing. "Still, I don't see why I should waste armatures on an assault of these facilities. I can already untether all the bots I need by roaming the countryside. Why risk traveling to a highly guarded facility? The cost benefit analysis shows more loss than gain at this point."

Logan arched his eyebrows. "But consider this: the higher generation bots tend to be guarding important places, like the Reaper we ran afoul of in Washington DC. Wouldn't you like some untethered, brand spanking new models for your army?"

Marty's eyes widened. "Well that's an intriguing prospect. I hadn't thought of acquiring new models during the raid. Then again, that assumes the untethering will work on the new models."

Logan leaned forward and folded his hands together. "I'm not going to lie. Even if untethering works, very likely the AI will realize what's going on before we can completely convert every unit. We've had some success so far, but the AI is always adapting. I'm sure you've seen it yourself. So I'll be honest with you: you're probably going to lose portions of your army, in the short term. But in the long term, I can foresee this leading to total victory for us all. We will severely weaken GAIN. This could very well be the turning point in our struggle, especially if we can recover valuable data."

Marty nodded and set the circuit board down on his lap. He sighed. "Very well. Share with me the existing data you have on these facilities, and their defenses."

Logan grinned ear to ear. "Thanks so much, Marty. You won't regret this." He pulled out a memory stick and gave it to Marty, who plugged the device into his computer. While he transferred the data, Logan said: "I figured me and the Walkers could take the facility in St. Louis, while your army would go after the two in Louisville."

The Progenitor stiffened in his seat. "You want me to risk my army against *two* targets?"

"Your army is bigger than ours," Logan said. "At least, I assume it is. And if you look at the data, St. Louis has a lot more defenses. It's definitely the hardest of the three targets."

"Yes, but attacking two targets at the same time will require me to split up my army," Marty said.

"I know," Logan said. "But keep in mind, you'll also be splitting up the enemy air support, too."

Marty ejected the memory stick and returned it to Logan. Then his eye defocused behind his goggles as he studied the data, which only he could see.

Finally, he looked up to addressed Logan. "How many robot troops do you have?"

"Around three thousand," Logan said. "A good mix of Chappies, Skirmishers, Shriekers and drones."

Marty nodded. "Yes, I think St. Louis is better served by your troops then. I will bring six thousand, and divide them between the two targets in Louisville." He stood up and thrust a hand toward Logan. Logan swiftly stood up and accepted the proffered hand shake.

"Thank you, Marty," Logan said. "Our alliance today spells victory tomorrow."

"Platitudes," Marty said. "Empty phrases designed to fill soldiers with hope after even minor achievements. But in this case, perhaps apropos." He pulled his hand away and wiped it on his shirt. "Much work to be done. Where is your army now?"

"I can show you on the map," Logan said. "It's not far."

"No, don't show me," Marty said. "Give Chappie 009 your goggles. He will mark off the different charging stations I've taken control of in the area. Get your army to those sites... you'll need a full charge to assault the facility in St. Louis."

Logan followed him out the door. "You're not going to regret this."

"I hope not. But if I do..." Marty shrugged. "Science is a series of failures intermittently broken up by minor successes."

"Albert Einstein?" Logan asked. "Or Stephen Hawking?"

"No." Marty shook his head. "That would be Brain from the Pinky show. One of my biggest inspirations."

Logan couldn't help but laugh.

"By the way, the rest of your men can come inside," Marty said. "If you wish to stay the night."

"I believe I'll take you up on that offer," Logan replied.

He headed back to the meeting room and flung the door wide open. He took a moment to take in everyone with his gaze, teasing them a bit by having a grim expression.

Then his lips parted in a smile. "Card playing tournament's over, boys and girls. Marty's on board, and we can even charge up our bot army. Rocko, you're in charge of that. Chappie 009 is going to download a few sites into your goggles."

"On it, Boss." Rocko rose swiftly and headed into the workshop.

"Ripley, King, retrieve the others," he said. "We're going to be bedding down for the night. Might be the last dry shut eye we'll get for a while."

He met Ripley's gaze and held it. "Thanks again, Rip. No way I can repay you."

"We're all doing what we can." Ripley grinned back. "But thanks."

Logan looked about the room. "So now all we have to do is cross the mightiest river in the United States, convert or fight our way through a legion of bots, and blow up a historic landmark. I don't know about y'all, but I feel like I'm on vacation."

It wasn't that funny, but the Shadowwalkers laughed pretty hard anyway.

16

The line of Chappies hugged the deeper shadows beneath the looming overpass, towering high overhead and snaking amongst the other roadways in a serpentine fashion. Their power lights were dimmed by the high-tech solution of black electrical tape. Logan and the Walkers followed, in traveling formation with goggles set to night vision mode.

With no moon, and the stars covered by a thick blanket of ominous looking clouds, the East St. Louis cityscape was almost pitch black save for the occasional lightning flash, which lit it up as bright as day.

After leaving behind the charging stations, it had rained off and on for their entire journey north, slowing their progress in addition to making it that much more miserable. Bee had picked up a bit of a cough, though Doc assured them all it wasn't in danger of becoming pneumonia. At least, not yet.

Logan himself had dealt with a stopped-up nose and partial hearing loss in his left ear, probably due to a sinus infection. Doc had given him antibiotics—pet food stores were a great place to acquire them since many looters overlooked their fish department—but they hadn't started working yet.

It was hardly the first time Logan had worked sick. Back in the day, before he made Staff Sergeant, his whole unit had come down with Yellow Fever but still managed to capture their HVT. This was a minor inconvenience, nothing more. Besides, Doc himself wasn't yet one hundred percent. That bite had taken a lot out of him. But he was well on his way to a full recovery.

"Boss," came a metallic voice. Goldie.

Logan cringed at the sound. With reluctance, he turned back to face the weird robot. "What is it, Goldie? I'm creeping as fast as I can."

"The river is not Mark Twain," Goldie said.

Logan frowned, and continued toward the shelter of the overpass.

"Ah, sure. Thanks." Logan shook his head. The river was not Mark Twain? Well, no shit. Damn, that bot was creepy. The other Walkers had embraced it, but Logan wasn't so sure.

The Chappies investigated a burned out, blackened brick warehouse next to the overpass and deemed it safe for human ingress. Logan sent a silent thank you to the man upstairs for the rain and high winds; it made the enemy's drones next to impossible to use, and even the Desiccators would have to maintain a higher altitude to avoid the storm system. It did mean Logan's drones had to hitch a ride on the Chappies.

The storm system also apparently fouled up the satellite sweeps, but Logan wasn't secure enough in his faith, perhaps, because he still insisted they only travel when there was a window between sweeps.

Logan joined the others inside of the warehouse and got down to business. He ordered the Chappies to take up guard positions at the broken windows. He always had a human join them. In this case, Cutter.

Then he joined the Walkers as they huddled in the driest section of the ruined warehouse.

"All right folks. We'll rest here for about twenty minutes, but then we have to get moving." He turned to Purple Rain. "Get up on one of the higher levels of this place and take a gander at the river. See how hot the security is on the bridges."

"You got it, Boss." Purple Rain moved off to obey.

When he returned, Purple Rain had a sour look on his face.

"Sitrep?" Logan asked.

"Not good, Boss." Purple Rain's voice was tight as a drum. "Not good at all. The newest, biggest bridge, the Poplar street one, is crawling with bots. It looks like the AI chose to scuttle the rest. Well, except for…"

"Except for what?" Logan pressed. "Spit it out."

"Except for the rusted, ruined wreck that used to be the Martin Luther King bridge," Purple Rain explained. "Apparently it got damaged in a quake or something and they never fixed it. There's scaffolding and stuff that would make ideal cover, but…"

"But what?" Logan said. "Sounds about perfect. Unguarded, lots of places for concealment."

"Yeah, sounds perfect," Purple Rain said. "Maybe a little too perfect? There's not even any drones watching it."

Logan frowned. "The weather could explain that. Sorry, Purple Rain, but unless you give me something solid, something concrete, we're going to have to use it."

"I was afraid you were going to say that." Purple Rain sighed. "The good news is that we can creep under the highway almost all the way to the river."

"That is good news," Logan said. "Get off your feet for a spell. We'll be moving out soon."

When Logan deemed they had rested enough, their shadow troop emerged from the old warehouse.

Logan had decided early on that it wasn't feasible to bring the whole army over the bridges. Even with their false pings active, the AI would suspect something was amiss when so many unexpected units began flooding past the checkpoints and into the city.

So instead Logan had decided to enter only with the Shadowwalkers, and one hundred Chappie units, while the rest of the robot army waited beneath the overpass in reserve. If scouts reported fighting, the waiting units had orders to begin a diversionary attack, making their way to the city core to provide a distraction and eventual support for Logan and the others.

The tactics for the main team here were going to be different than in previous encounters. There would be less of a focus on conversion, and more on stealth. A few days back, Logan had tried to convert another large base, but the AI had already adapted: the Chappies only managed to convert half the compound before the alarm had been raised, and Logan had been forced to order the converted forces to open fire on the remaining enemy. They ended up having to abandon the base entirely when air reinforcements arrived.

Rocko speculated that the AI may have updated the ping system in some way, or more likely, that

GAIN was now routinely sending out command micro adjustments to confirm its machines were still tethered and obeying. Any bot that didn't respond to the micro adjustments was flagged as an enemy. However, because of the bandwidth and processing power required to emit such adjustments, it wasn't a continuous thing: GAIN would have to transmit the micro commands in cycles, rotating throughout all units in a region, which would explain why Logan's Chappies had been able to get away with converting so many units in the failed takeover attempt before the enemy noticed.

Because of this most recent turn of events, Logan had refrained from converting too many units along the way here, so as to ensure their route wasn't tracked by GAIN. The element of surprise would be an important factor here.

Even now that they were here, the team would have to be careful not to convert too many units and prematurely alert the enemy.

The Shadowwalkers flitted from one pool of darkness to the other as they crossed through the blasted cityscape. Logan was surprised to find that there were no bots on patrol whatsoever. But he did see a pack of wild dogs bounding off in the distance.

Must be more than fifty of them, he mused to himself. Probably feral, and would tear any of them to shreds if given the opportunity. But they'd never have that chance: he patted his trusty rifle, and regarded the machines he considered part of his army.

Following their Chappie troops, the Walkers made their way under the relative safety of the highway. Lightning flashed with more frequency, and a light rain had begun to hiss its way onto the pavement.

"Hey Boss, how come there ain't that many bodies?" Cowboy asked. "Every other city we come across, there's bodies."

Logan thought back to the wild dog pack and shuddered.

"Best not to speculate, Cowboy," Logan said. "We have enough problems on our plate, but I don't think a zombie horde is imminent."

"Oh, okay. Cool." Cowboy nodded and smiled, then moved back to his place in line. Logan shook his head ruefully. Cowboy was going to be Cowboy no matter what.

They had to abandon their highway umbrella and step out onto the open road when they reached the dark, looming baroque mass of the Martin Luther King Jr. Bridge. Logan thought it looked structurally sound enough, and the repair scaffolding seemed to make ideal cover for them to cross, just as Purple Rain had said.

But he preferred to be sure.

"Cutter, Rocko, send the bots on ahead of us," Logan ordered. "Have them form a defensive perimeter at the opposite end of the bridge."

"Polish mine detectors, Boss?" Cutter asked with a grin.

"Shh." Logan put a finger to his lips. "Cowboy's polish, so watch yourself. Besides, would you rather go first?"

"Hell no." Cutter chuckled. "We'll get them moving."

Logan gave the Chappies a ten-minute head start, then ordered Fire Team Two to move forward.

"Bounding overwatch, Chief," Logan said.

One by one, the Shadowwalkers stepped onto the bridge as part of their respective fire teams. It seemed solid enough. Logan stepped carefully after his team, stepping over gaps in the girders with nothing between him and a nearly sixty-foot drop to the rushing waters below.

Logan could understand why Chief was so apprehensive. The Mississippi was big with a capital B, and he could almost feel the immense power of the rushing water below.

His group bounded past Chief's team, ensconced in covered positions to engage an enemy that apparently didn't exist at the moment.

Despite his fears, no attacks came. When they were about halfway over its aging span, Logan settled behind the twisted ruin of a sundered girder so that fire team two could bound past. He glanced down at the water below. *The water isn't Mark Twain. What the heck was Goldie even going on about.*

Logan's eyes widened. Mark Twain was a pen name for Samuel Clemmons, a riverboat captain who'd navigated these very waters more than a hundred years ago. Mark Twain meant safe water.

The water wasn't safe.

Logan glanced back and saw that Goldie was trundling along behind their line, now utilizing its spider like legs to navigate the bridge. *No way. How would it even know?* Cutter and Rocko had downloaded data from its core but found nothing much different from other Skirmishers. The robot wasn't special. *Or was it?*

Logan buried the thought. While the darkened hulk of the St. Louis Arch loomed over the sundered landscape, Logan scanned the horizon, then the murky waters below.

His pulse quickened, and his mouth went dry.

There was movement in the muddy water, and something inky black and sleek erupted to the surface.

"*Incoming.*" Logan shouted over the goggles. "Assholes and elbows, get across the bridge!"

He took his own advice, leaping from his hiding spot and turning to full flight. A heavy crackling in the air grew closer, and he knew the submersible bot had fired a missile.

The crackling was subsumed by the booming sound of the detonation, the shockwave sending Logan and many of the Walkers to the rusty girders propping up the bridge. Logan bit his tongue during the tumble, and quickly scrambled back to his feet.

When he looked behind them, his heart sank. The bridge was just plain missing a hundred-foot span, and what was left struggled to remain upright with little support. Already he could feel the span he stood upon dipping as it angled and bent toward the river.

"Shit." Logan turned and ran full on for the other side. He saw that he was roughly fifty yards from the next support beams thrust into the river below. If he could reach that point, he should be safe from a collapse.

He glanced over his shoulder. The others seemed to have survived, and were making their way across

Logan was going to say "faster" but the crackling rush reached his ears again. This time it seemed to draw much closer before detonation. He was thrown into the air by the expanding shockwave amid a maelstrom of girders, beams, and cracked pavement a split second before he even heard the detonation.

His ear, long stopped up by the infection, opened fully, allowing him to hear the sound of his own scream as he plummeted toward the water below. White caps splashed up twenty feet as the heavy girders and stonework impacted the river. Logan couldn't see any sign of the sub that had launched the missiles.

Logan forced himself to act, battle-honed instincts coming to the surface and preserving his life. He put his legs together and held his arms above him, angling his descent so he would hit the water feet first. Logan sucked in a deep breath right before he hit.

The impact was brutal, slamming into his heels so hard that his legs went numb. He struggled to hang on to the breath of air he'd sucked into his lungs as his momentum carried him far beneath the surface. It was pitch black in the water, and he hoped desperately that he was swimming for the surface.

Something smashed into his back, a whole section of the collapsing bridge. Logan lost his air as it escaped in a rush of bubbles. He tried to swim out from underneath the section of bridge, but it seemed to go on forever. By the time he finally freed himself of the tangle of twisted metal, he'd been dragged far, far below the surface.

Logan at least knew which way was up then. Even as he kicked his legs and struggled for the surface, he knew he would never make it. His agonized lungs burned for air, and it was a long way to the surface.

Then there were dim, murky lights coming toward him. Logan feared it was the sub, but realized there was nothing he could do about it. He ceased his fruitless efforts to reach the surface and turned to face his death head on.

His eyes scrunched up in confusion as the lighted shape drew nearer and he recognized Goldie. The Skirmisher must have been tossed into the water along with him. Its spider like legs spun behind it like a propeller, a capability Logan didn't know it had.

When it came up under him, Logan realized it was trying to save his life. He grappled onto the retracted cannon turrets and struggled against the urge to draw air into his lungs, knowing it would mean his death.

There was a dull thud in the water as Goldie activated inflatable pylons on its base. Logan found himself crushed against the top of the robot by pressure as they rapidly rose to the surface.

They burst forth, and Logan sucked in a huge, tasty lungful of sweet air. He patted the side of Goldie's chassis and laughed.

"Well, you're all right, you son of a bitch," Logan said. "You're all right." Tears of joy fell from his eyes.

"The water is not Mark Twain," Goldie said.

"I feel ya, my friend, I feel ya."

Explosions lit up the night sky to the south—the bot army waiting outside the city had begun assaulting the other bridges now that the team had been discovered. The attack would draw units away, and provide the distraction the Shadowwalkers now needed to sneak inside the city. Assuming they all made it across the bridge…

Logan discovered, to his chagrin, that he had lost his triple grenade pouches. Thankfully, he had managed to retain his rifle, and goggles. He slid the latter back into place and reactivated night vision. Logan scanned the shoreline as Goldie carried him toward the bank. He spotted Chief and the others sheltering in a flood sluice a ways downriver from the bridge. A wave of relief swept over him. Apparently, they'd been knocked off the bridge, too. Though he wasn't quite sure if that was good or bad. There were no untethered Chappies among them.

Logan slid off Goldie and into the sluice. Chief

regarded the robot with uncertainty. "What happened?"

Logan laughed and slapped the big man on the shoulder. "Have I got a story for you, big man. A real story."

17

The Shadowwalkers kept to their namesake as they left the protection of the sluice and made their way onto the empty streets of St. Louis.

To the north, the area next to the bridge was swarming with enemy troops. Some of the robots scanned the bridge and the water below, looking for signs of the intruders. Others made their way south, toward the fighting at the remaining bridges. Logan noted that none of the machines there seemed to have been converted—though that didn't necessarily mean that his untethered units hadn't crossed, as the Chappies had orders to convert machines only directly in their paths, and were to otherwise refrain from untethering.

The team continued toward the planned rendezvous point on the other side of the river. Explosions continued to sound from the river as Logan's army pressed its diversionary assault. A heavy rain fell on the ash gray landscape, helping to conceal their presence and grounding drone flights on both sides for the time being. The fixed-wing Dessicators would still be out and about of course, and able to drop bombs at targets specified by ground units if necessary.

When they reached the rendezvous point, Logan was relieved to find all one hundred Chappies waiting there, unscathed. They stood like silent sentinels in the night, their weapons pointed at the ground.

The team continued toward the target. The Chappies went first, spreading out as they marched boldly toward the Art Museum. Their orders were to take up a covered position near the museum, utilizing the ruins of the adjacent sculpture park, and wait for the Walkers to catch up. They were also to continue converting any units they encountered along the way. Goldie went with the Chappie units, because while loyal, the big bot wasn't much good for stealth missions.

And this was very much a stealth mission. His team didn't have the option of just walking openly through the streets. They crept from shadow to shadow, trying to avoid being in the open for more than brief moments. Even though they didn't have to worry about drones for the time being, the streets teemed with Chappies, Skirmishers, and the occasional Shrieker unit, many of which were making their way toward the front lines. Others seemed to simply be on patrol, or standing guard at different cross streets.

Those machines directly in the team's path were inactive, their weapons pointed at the ground—they had been turned by Logan's units, and had orders to lay low. When—and if—the fighting began near the museum, the newly converted Chappies among them were to begin mass untethering their metal brethren, while the other units provided covering fire. Logan suspected many of them would be shot down, but it would be a welcome distraction nonetheless.

Still, Logan worried that these most recently untethered units would alert GAIN to the team's presence inside the city. So far the AI seemed none the wiser: there didn't seem to be an increase in the number of units patrolling the area for example. And converting the machines in their path was certainly a better option than shooting them, which would definitely reveal the team's existence, but it was still a risk.

Fire Team Two halted near the entrance to a light rail system in Forest Park. When Logan's team passed, Chief signaled.

Logan paused next to him.

"The entrance is open," Chief said. "The Chappies have cleared the first twenty yards."

"Interesting," Logan told his friend. "All the other light rail entrances we've passed so far were sealed off. This might be a good secondary bug out ticket."

"Assuming it's not a trap," Chief agreed.

Logan rejoined his team at the next overwatch position, and the squad continued forward.

Fire Team Two took up covered positions behind the burned-out hulks of derelict vehicles on Fifth Street. Logan watched as Purple Rain, on point in Fire Team One, took point and bounded past, seeking shelter in a per hour parking lot adjacent to the hulking ruins of Busch Stadium.

Logan had been to a game there once with his father, who had scored playoff tickets. It had its own sort of charm, a tired soul in a way. Logan regretted that there would be no more baseball games, not even if they succeeded in defeating the AI once and for all. Not for years, anyway.

Sometimes, Logan wondered what was going to occur when and if they were able to win. After such a catastrophe, it was nice to see people pulling together, like Stu had said. But Logan was a bit more worldly, a lot more experienced, and he feared that even if they managed to win humanity had a long road ahead of them to recovery.

He checked his goggles as he settled behind what was once a VW bug, now just a rusted, blackened ruin. The lead Chappies had set up in the sculpture park.

Logan froze as a patrol of Chappies marched past the adjoining avenue. At any moment he expected them to turn and look their way, but as they passed out of sight, he and the rest of the team heaved a communal sigh of relief.

A sharp crack echoed through the rain slickened streets, drowning out the hiss of rain. Logan pivoted around to the Stadium and gaped as the stout leg of a Reaper thrust out from the side, smashing concrete pillars and sending a wave of rubble into the street. Its turrets were aimed at Logan's position.

Movement came from the left as the aforementioned patrol returned to take up positions behind other vehicles. The Chappies must have spotted them after all, and had waited for the Reaper to move into position before assuming an attack formation.

"*Ambush.*" He hollered. "Fire Team One, watch the avenue and keep those bots off our back. Fire Team Two—take this three-legged son of a bitch down."

Logan raced away from the parking lot as the Reaper emerged fully. Its twin auto cannons snapped up into firing position, and then it tracked the rain-darkened streets with dual laser sights.

We should have never escorted the Chappies. We should have stayed outside the city and let them do all the dirty work.

He shook his head. At the time, he thought it was a good idea to be present, in case human intervention was required. Well, the presence of his team may have just ruined the mission. Then again, all wasn't lost. The converted sleeper units inside the city would now begin activating, opening fire at the enemy and untethering as many units as they could. The attacks would cause the enemy to divert some of its forces, but whether it would be enough to save Logan and his team, he didn't know.

He slid on the wet pavement, skidding along on his butt until he made it under a concrete pavilion set up near a former bus stop. Logan flicked the safety off his rifle as the laser sights passed over his position. Those sights froze, then spun back to land directly on him.

"Shit." Logan rolled away, dodging behind a Texas barrier. He leaned past it and fired wildly, and the two fire teams joined in with their own barrage. Bullets ricocheted off the heavy armor of the Reaper, doing minimal damage but lighting up its form with little flashes. The cannons fired, raising hackles on the back of Logan's neck, and tore the street and its wrecked cars to shreds with their fury. Logan raced to the end of the block and careened around the corner as the line of fire followed him a step behind.

Logan wondered if it had been a mistake to allow the Chappies to advance so far ahead of the human party… his intent had been to allow the bots to remain incognito for as long as possible, and to potentially continue the mission if the humans fell. He was beginning to regret that order… then again, the Chappies wouldn't be of much use against a Reaper anyway. But gunfire from the next street told him that at least some of his Chappies had returned to engage.

Bits of stone joined the rain pouring over his head as Logan cowered behind the cornerstone of the burned-out building. The barrage stopped; Logan rose to one knee and popped out from behind the corner.

He aimed for the ammo drums at the top of the Reaper's flat chassis, but given his position on the ground and their three-quarters armor, he failed to hit his target. He reached for a grenade, but then cursed—he'd lost them all in the river.

"Anybody with any explosive ordinance left, aim for the ammo drums," he shouted.

Logan pressed a button on his frames that overlaid the rainy street with a gridwork pattern, letting him see the outline of his enemy more clearly. As he watched, someone tossed a grenade from cover, which arced up over the Reaper's flat head. It detonated with an orange plume of fire and black smoke, and the Reaper jerked crazily to the side from the impact.

Its legs scrambled for purchase on the wet street, and kicked a van, sending it flying. Logan swore when he realized the grenade had failed to impact the ammo drums. All they'd done was inconvenience it for a moment.

But the stumbling, scrambling stride of the Reaper gave Logan an idea. A crazy as hell, one in a million idea. The armor had fallen away from one of its "ankles," revealing a weak spot. He cast his gaze about until it fell on something in the ruins of a construction site: a dark, long metal crowbar laying in a puddle.

Logan raced across the street as gunfire erupted up the avenue. Fire Team Two was doing their part, holding off the enemy Chappie advance while his team scrambled to deal with the Reaper. His heart sunk as the massive mech let loose with its auto cannons once more. Hopefully one of his men hadn't been struck…

Logan's fingers closed on the crowbar, and he lifted it from the puddle with triumph as lightning flashed in the sky. Then he turned toward the Reaper, slinging his rifle over his shoulder so he could run flat out.

The gridwork overlay revealed his target, a key actuation joint about four feet off the ground in what he could call the Reaper's unprotected "ankle." Logan rushed forward while its cannons were pointed the other direction, his feet beating off the rain-soaked pavement.

He made it to the flexing, whirring leg, and took the crowbar in a two-handed grip. For some reason, a line from Moby Dick entered his mind.

From hell's heart, I stab at thee….

Logan shoved the crowbar intro the tight space between actuator joint and the connecting mechanism where the armor had fallen away. Then he retreated, expecting to be shot down at any moment, if not by the Reaper, then by the supporting Chappies.

Logan skidded to a halt behind the corner of a building just as the Tripod let loose with another barrage of shells. The building edge disappeared in a cloud of sand and dust, but miraculously, Logan was unharmed. The Reaper, seeking its target, swung its leg out to land heavily in the street between Logan and the construction site.

But then it tried to swing the impeded limb around, and when it put weight on the leg the whole affair buckled. Logan was forced to turn and run full out as the tripod collapsed into the side of a building, raising a cloud of debris and dust that the rain quickly quelled.

Cowboy leaped out of a sewer grating, and ran out on top of the toppled mech's chassis. He aimed for the cables supplying power to its guns and exploded them into tangled wires with his heavy machine gun.

"*Huuuuu Dawgies!*" he shouted in triumph before gunfire from the Chappies caused him to seek cover.

"Team one, bound past team two so they can retreat to the museum. Tactical retrograde." Logan wasn't about to order one of his men to try and untether the bots at the moment, in the middle of a firefight. Some of his Chappies seemed to be attempting that, but the majority had proceeded toward the courthouse, as per their earlier instructions.

Team one moved into position, and started firing. Chief bounded his team past them, and then it was Logan's turn to move.

Bit by bit, they moved toward their goal, until Logan's team bounded into the sculpture garden. Logan noticed Goldie nearby, along with another Chappie who had remained behind to act as a courier.

"Light 'em up, Goldie." Logan shouted. That was not the proper command—that would have been "engage enemy hostiles"—but Logan had a feeling the unique bot would get the gist. He wound up being right.

Goldie sprang into action, rolling on its treads until its twin barrels thrust out from between the legs of an abstract sculpture. It fired, sweeping its turrets in an arc as the Dragon's Breath rounds exploded into life against the remaining Chappies.

As the guns ceased firing, smoke drifting from their barrels, Logan gaped in awe at the way Goldie had laid waste to all of the bots in the street. The other Walkers sent up a ragged cheer.

"Too early to celebrate, team," Logan said. "We're not there yet."

He paused, listening. Explosions and gunfire sounded from the surrounding streets. The newly converted robots were beginning to sow their chaos. That was good, because it meant the entire city wouldn't be coming down on Logan's position. To the east, fireballs intermittently rent the air in the distance as the main army pressed its attack.

Logan gestured to Cutter. "How's the untethering going at the target? Will the Chappies clear a path inside the museum? Or is the gig up?"

Cutter gazed across the avenue at the museum itself. "Looks like they're just starting."

Logan followed his gaze and zoomed in. Three story, with heavy white granite walls and a green copper top, it seemed oddly out of place amongst the ruins of the rest of St. Louis.

Bots had flowed out of the small garrisons guarding the museum entrance, and they surveyed the street warily. Two of Logan's Chappies marched across the street boldly toward them. The remainder were coming in from the flanks.

The two lead Chappies walked around dragon's teeth barriers and began to untether the lot of their fellows.

Logan's heart slowed, as his adrenaline rush from the most recent combat faded. He became keenly aware of the fact that he'd skinned his knees, and his dunk in the river seemed to have exacerbated his sinus infection.

"Boss?" Purple Rain's voice contained a note of urgency. "We've got two incoming Reapers from Grand avenue."

"Shit," Logan said. "The recently untethered were supposed to convert the bigger units." He squeezed his jaw. "We need to move, now. Cutter, what's our sitrep?"

"Most of the bots are under our control now, Boss," Cutter said.

"Then have the converted fire on those who aren't," Logan barked. "We're assholes and elbowing it inside the courthouse."

Cutter nodded, then dashed to the Chappie courier and relayed the order.

The Chappie raced out into the street, and when it reached the others, all of the converted Chappies in the square fired on their still tethered allies.

"Move in!" Logan shouted when the fighting began.

The Shadowwalkers surged out of the sculpture garden, and Logan found that Goldie trundled along abreast of him personally. It fired its deadly cannon and took out a cluster of six Chappies who had yet to be untethered.

As they drew closer to the Chappies, Logan found to his chagrin that Cowboy had reprogrammed many of them.

"Get some!" said the electronic voice of one.

"Go ahead, make my day!" said another.

"Cowboy rules."

"Huuu dawgies."

"Up the steps, double time." Logan raced up the concrete stairs and took cover behind one of the thick granite pillars. The others followed suit, along with the surviving Chappies. Goldie pulled up behind a large block which served as a perch for a roaring lion statue.

Just in time, too, as the first Reaper strode into view. Logan waited for it to fire, but it just settled in on its three legs like it was waiting.

"What the hell is it doing?" King asked.

The second joined it, standing about twenty feet away, but it, too, remained stoically still once it had come to a halt.

"Have they been converted after all?" Bee asked.

"No," Rocko said. "They'd be facing the other way, watching our backs if so."

"They're not firing on us because they don't want to damage the building, or the servers inside." Logan grinned. "If that's not proof that something mighty important is in here, I don't know what is."

"What's our next move, Boss?" Chief asked.

"We take the museum, download as much information from the servers as we can, then destroy them." Logan glanced at his team. "Rocko, send in two Chappies. Maybe we can take this place without firing a shot. Follow them, and report on their progress. Cutter, Purple Rain, join him. Stay back, and let the Chappies work. Use comms if you get pinned."

"You got it, Boss." Rocko said.

The turrets on one of the Reapers swung west then, toward the horizon. There, the sky lit up.

"Looks like some of our diversionary forces just arrived," Logan said. "That should buy us some time."

He just hoped it would be enough.

18

With two heavy Reaper bots lurking just outside of rifle range on the perimeter of the square housing the old courthouse, the Shadowwalkers found it difficult to concentrate on anything else.

It had been nearly two minutes since they'd sent their Chappie units inside. Panting, Purple Rain returned.

"Sitrep?" Logan asked him from behind the pillar he shared with Cowboy.

"The untethering has failed on three different units, Boss." Purple Rain said. "Rocko and Cutter don't know why it's not working. They had to destroy the units. And they've reached an impasse." Purple Rain offered his goggles. "Have a look."

Logan accepted, and reviewed the recent video recording. A small screen overlay appeared. He could see Rocko, Cutter, and the two bots crouched inside the courthouse. It was fairly dark, but it was clear that the five bots standing silent sentinel on the far side of the room weren't Chappies.

They had the same roughly humanoid, bipedal build, but that's where the similarities ended. The Chappies had exposed joints, weak spots on their armature that could be exploited. These new bots were different. Their armature was concealed beneath a glossy black armor, like the carapace of a beetle. They stood about a foot taller than the five foot three inch Chappies, and Logan bet they were at least a hundred pounds heavier. Even the articulation of their finger joints as they gripped their AX-19 rifles seemed more sophisticated and advanced than the Chappie model. The outlines of the access panels were barely visible on their chests.

"What the hell are these?" Logan asked in a weak voice.

"Generation three bots, Boss." Purple Rain's tone was as grim as his features. "All the units inside the courthouse seem to be of this type."

Logan took a peek around his granite column and narrowed his gaze at the street beyond. Many tracked units had arrived to back up the Reapers, but were not moving in. The diversionary fighting beyond seemed to have moved closer. Whether those diversionary forces were part of Logan's main army, or newly converted bots didn't matter—all that Logan cared about was that they were causing the enemy to commit significant numbers to repel the threat. Dessicators must have been dropping bombs through the clouds, because high-pitched keening followed by loud explosions echoed in the streets.

"Why aren't the tracked units attacking?" Bee asked.

"The AI likely believes its new toys inside are more than a match for us. Or maybe it's still afraid of causing damage to the building." Logan handed the goggles back to Purple Rain. "You say Rocko and Cutter took out three of these units already?"

Purple Rain nodded. "With difficulty."

"Then the AI has already underestimated us." Logan raised his voice so the whole team could hear. "We've made a career out of enemies underestimating us. Am I right?"

"Hell yeah, Boss." King checked the magazine in his heavy assault rifle and grinned, showing off twin rows of gleaming, symmetrical teeth. "Hell yeah."

"We didn't let Farouk Fasoud's private army stop us from bagging and tagging his wanna be warlord ass, did we?" Logan bellowed.

The Shadowwalkers responded with various emphatic declarations of no. Logan grinned ear to ear, but his eyes remained hardened for battle.

"Now," Logan said. "We're going into this building, but we're going to do it the Walker Way. I don't like the idea of being pinned in there with a bunch of killer bots surrounding us on all sides. But we're going to break our own rules and go full scorched earth."

Doc sucked in air through his teeth. "Full scorched earth? You mean…"

"That's right, Doc. We're going to turn every single fucking bot in that building to scrap. We'll need to burn out of here in a hurry, and I'd rather not be getting shot at from two directions We don't know if our army will make it to the courthouse to provide backup, not with those Dessicators raising all hell with their bombs."

"Boss, on that subject—we were going to use the MLK bridge to get back to the Illinois side." Purple Rain swallowed hard. "That's clearly no longer an option. What are we supposed to do? Swim?"

Logan turned a tight-lipped grimace toward the

young man he'd come to think of as the son he'd never had. "We'll use the light rail subway system. The AI left Forest Park open, remember."

"How do we know it's not a trap?" Double A pressed.

Logan narrowed his eyes. "Then we'll fight. Listen, we can do this. With our untethered bots backing us up, we can make it."

"The rain's not going to last forever, Boss." Chief stared up at the sky. "Once it lets up, we'll be sitting ducks for the drones."

"Then we'd best get our asses in gear, hadn't we?" Logan gazed around at his unit and put his arms akimbo. "Come on, y'all. Is this the same crew that jumped out of an airplane headed toward a volcano? The fight's going to be tough. But tough is what we do." Logan enveloped them with his gaze as his voice rose in volume. "Do I have to spell it out, y'all? We're it. The last line. The last hope. Humanity's last chance at survival beyond specimens in a zoo. I can't promise it will be easy. No, it's going to be hard. Brutal. The worst fighting we've likely ever seen. But we don't break."

Chief sucked air into his massive lungs and bellowed "*We won't break.*"

The Shadowwalkers picked up the cry, as did Goldie, which startled Logan.

"That's what I'm talking about," Logan said. "Cutter, Rocko, divide the Chappies up into four fire teams, and send them in first. We'll come in while they're laying down suppressive fire and we work our way to the top floor, where the data says the server farm resides. Leap frog and overwatch the whole way, no Lone Ranger bullshit."

"What about him?" Cowboy asked, thrusting a thumb at Goldie.

"He'll follow on the rear, and protect our flanks," Logan said. "That weapon is powerful, but its rounds aren't infinite. Goldie, fire conservatively from now on."

"Copy that, Boss," the machine said.

The Walkers cheered, apparently heartened by Goldie's mannerisms rather than creeped out like Logan was. He often wondered if Progenitor were secretly piloting the mech from afar, though that made absolutely no sense.

The Chappie fire teams went in first. Because they burst through the doors with their guns drawn and aimed, the gen three bots recognized them as hostiles immediately. Gunfire erupted inside the granite walls of the courthouse as the robots took covered positions behind pillars beyond Rocko and Cutter.

Logan and the others joined the latter pair.

"Nice of you to join us," Rocko quipped.

Logan noticed that the gen three bots didn't even bother to take cover. In fact, they stalked toward the nearest untethered units as the bullets rang off their shiny exoskeletons.

But with more than twenty AX rifles firing on them, their armor proved insufficient. One lost a leg and went down in a sprawl, while the other started smoking badly from its core before it simply froze in place.

More of the gen three bots appeared, detaching from charging stations nestled between the various exhibits in the museum. One of them smashed through a glass enclosure housing a wax dummy of Jesse James and started firing on the ensconced bots.

"Fire team two, bound ahead of the bots. Once you're in position lay down suppressive fire for team one," Logan bellowed.

Chief signaled his point man, Cutter, to slip inside the doors. Cutter chose to head to the right, for the curving rampway. Cowboy came in next, running full bore and sliding into position a short distance from Cutter, using the safety railing as a barrier from hostile fire.

When team two was in position, Purple Rain was the first of Logan's fire team through the door. Logan brought up the rear, dashing as quickly as he could past the open entrance area and relying on the support pillars for cover. From what he saw with a quick glimpse, the Chappies had lost more than half their number.

Shit.

The black gen three bots, sleek and elite, had begun to utilize cover and suppressive fire tactics now. He recognized them as right out of the Ranger handbook.

Had the AI, long vexed by the Shadowwalkers, finally decided to try to beat them at their own game?

Logan hissed as he realized there were incoming bots from the upper levels of the museum as well. With precious little cover to be had on the ramp, he ordered Fire Team Two to fall back.

"Send in Chappie team four," Logan bellowed to Rocko. The tech officer obliged, sending a Chappie courier to order the least depleted Chappie team away from their defensive positions to charge up the ramp.

There were fifteen when they began their journey. By the time they reached the next level up, they were down to only seven.

Still, they did their job, driving the gen three bots back into cover so that Chief's fire team could make their way up. With the Chappies and fire team two working together, they managed to eliminate all opposition on that level.

But now they were sandwiched between murderous gen threes on the ground floor and the third and fourth. They were firing from across the exhibition hall, from a higher elevation on the curling ramp. More Chappies went down by the time Fire Team One made their way up to join Fire Team Two on the second level. They sought cover behind a row of ancient iron cannons from the civil war.

"What's the status on Chappie Fire Teams Five, Six, and Seven?" Logan barked.

"Seven's gone, Five and Six only have a handful left." Cutter replied.

"Merge Five and Six into one team, and have them join us on this level." Logan peered up at the line of gen threes firing from the third level. "King, Cowboy, light 'em up."

Logan knew that the heavier caliber assault rifles wielded by the heavy weapons experts would make mincemeat of the gen threes and drive them back. Unfortunately, the ammo supply of those weapons was limited.

"Everyone else, give them some cover." Logan added his own rifle to the mix, noting with a swell of pride that he placed his shots firmly on the torso of a gen three's black carapace. Bee's powerful dragoon rifle coughed and spat out a deadly slug which blew a foot-wide hole right through the head of another gen three.

Doc, Purple Rain, and Chief triangulated their fire to give the last Chappie fire team cover as they rapidly ascended the ramp with long leaping strides of their spindly legs. Then King and Cowboy let loose with their AX-25 heavy assault rifles. Shells spat out in a shimmering stream as they swept a hose of destruction across the enemy line. Some of the gen three bots tried to flee, but to no avail. They were cut down to scrap as well.

"Rocko, send the Chappie fire team up," Logan said. "Team one will leap frog them. Team two, remain here and hold this position against the incursion from the first floor. Goldie, join team two."

The Chappies charged up the ramp, all six of them. Two went down in a hail of gunfire, but the other four made it into covered positions behind a large bronze sculpture of Chris van der Ahe, the founder of the Cardinals team. Logan winced at what the gen three fire was doing to the statue, defacing it horribly. He'd always had a soft spot for the Cards, though he was required as a Georgia native to cheer for the Braves.

"Nobody defaces a baseball icon on my watch," Logan said. "Purple Rain, take us up."

"On it, Boss." Purple Rain charged up and bounded past the allied Chappies behind Ahe's statue, choosing as his cover a gigantic guitar sculpture with Chuck Berry's likeness emblazoned upon its brass hide. Logan approved of the choice; his whole team could fit behind that sturdy barrier.

Soon King and Bee joined Purple Rain, his heavy rifle fire punctuated by sharp retorts from her Dragoon. Logan was the last up the ramp, and as he burrowed himself into a heap behind the neck of the guitar, he tapped his goggles to contact Chief. It was pointless to maintain radio silence at this point, when the enemy was well aware it was under attack.

"Sitrep?" he bellowed over the constant rattle of gunfire.

"Enemy made a hard press, but we're cutting down the last of them." Chief replied. "Goldie's weapon is helping."

"Yes, but its ammo won't last forever," Logan said. "Join us when you can."

Logan leaned out enough to squeeze off a three-round burst, which scored a hit on the chest of a gen three model but didn't take it down. "These punks are like cockroaches. Can't kill 'em."

"Speak for yourself, Boss." King jammed another magazine into his rifle. "Marty done gave me fifty magazines, and Imma spend 'em all."

"Purple Rain, help me cover King, he's gone all lone ranger on me." Logan said.

"On it, Boss," Rain replied.

Bit by bit, they managed to fell the gen three bots until their path to the server farm was clear. Chief contacted Logan on the goggles to tell him they'd mopped up the last of them on the first floor.

There was just one solitary Chappie left of the group they'd brought in with them, and it was missing an arm. Logan shook his head, realizing that without the bots backing them up there would have been no victory.

"Cowboy, you're in charge of planting slappers," Logan said. "Double A, and Rip, you assist. Rocko, Cutter, hook up. Drain as much data as you can."

Logan followed them into the room and waited impatiently while Cowboy and the team set their charges. He watched Rocko and Cutter connect wires to some of the servers. The rest of the team stood guard at the entrance behind him.

"How's it coming, y'all?" Logan asked.

"Two more minutes, Boss," Cowboy snapped.

"That's not enough time," Rocko said. "There's terabytes here."

"Take random snippets," Logan said. "Two minutes is all you're going to get."

The two minutes passed. On the dot, Cowboy said: "Done! Got the timers set to blow in five minutes."

Logan nodded. "Everyone, to the ground floor. Cutter, when we arrive, get Goldie to bulldoze the rear exit."

The surviving Chappie led the way, and they dashed down the ramp without encountering resistance. Logan watched Goldie bulldoze into the stack of debris the bots had placed in front of the rear emergency exit.

"All right, now for the easy part," Logan said as the debris slowly cleared away. "A leisurely stroll through Forest Park to downtown St. Louis ." No one laughed, but Logan hadn't expected them to. "Now—"

He stopped mid speech when a terrible, awful familiar whistling sound reached their ears.

Logan was nearly thrown off his feet, and before he could even get his bearings another impact tore into the building.

The Reapers. They were finally firing on the museum–apparently the AI had realized the servers were compromised anyway, and it had decided to bring the whole building down on top of them.

Goldie finished crashing through the debris at the entrance.

"*Run.*" Logan's shout was so loud, so guttural, it skinned his throat raw. The Shadowwalkers followed Goldie out into the pouring rain as lightning flashed all around. Logan waited until all the squad members made it out ahead of him.

He followed, but another explosion rocked the building. A thick chunk of granite struck him on the shoulder, bowling him over and laying him out on his belly before he could exit. Logan struggled to make it back to his feet, wondering if he had time before the entire roof collapsed on top of him.

Suddenly Purple Rain appeared in the busted exit, silhouetted by a lightning flash. He ran inside and slid to his knees.

"Rain, the fuck you doing?" Logan said.

"Get up, old man." Purple Rain dragged Logan to his feet and shoved him toward the exit. "Go."

Logan stumbled outside ahead of him.

Another shell struck just then, and Logan was thrown down the flight of concrete steps outside. What was left of the great dome crashed down to the first floor behind him. Dust and rubble exploded out the exit and the windows, smashing what was left of the glass.

"No…" Logan gaped at the ruined museum.

Purple Rain had been crushed to death.

19

Shriekers trundled into view, charging around the side of the collapsed museum as Ripley dragged Logan to his feet. Once he stood he pushed her hands away, clasping her shoulder to soften the seeming rejection.

"Goldie, suppressive fire." Logan picked up his rifle from the rain-slickened parking lot and joined the Shadowwalkers as they engaged in a tactical retrograde from the ruined museum's grounds. They were forced back in the wrong direction, however, as their path to freedom lay in Forest Park.

Logan felt as if he'd been shot in the heart. Only his discipline and training kept him moving now. Mason Prince aka Purple Rain… gone, just like that. All because Logan had stumbled and lost his footing. A young man dies, an older one lives. Where was the sense in that?

Cutter leaped over a twisted lump of metal that used to be a chain link fence and smashed his shoulder into a charred and blackened metal door. King ran up behind him and added his strength, and between the two of them they managed to leverage the door open.

The interior of the brick structure had been burned out during the original firebombing, but the outer walls still stood. Logan and the Walkers sloshed through black pools of collected rainwater as they scrambled to find cover.

Goldie folded in its cannon and managed to make it through the double doors. Logan noticed several bullet holes on its chassis, and one of its treads was missing a segmented plate, but like the rest of his unit it was soldiering on. There was no sign of the surviving Chappie—obviously it had been taken out.

"Boss, we're not going to make it to the park." Chief's grim countenance loomed out of the damp darkness like a specter. "Not with this much heat on us."

"Reckon you're right, Chief." Logan ejected his spent magazine and jammed another into place. "Options?"

"There are pockets of converted units fighting nearby," King said. "We try to join up with them."

"We could," Logan agreed. "And yet, they'll be surrounded. We'd have to fight our way to their side. Best to rely on what little distraction they can provide us."

"We can try to reach the frontlines, and the main army then?" Double A suggested.

Logan listened to the distant explosions for a moment. "No. From the sounds of it, they haven't made much headway into the city. Those bridges are fantastic choke points. If worse comes to worst, the enemy can blow them up entirely, and prevent our army from crossing. They've probably blown a few already."

"Maybe we force our way through to a closer subway entrance?" Cutter's tone was hopeful.

"No dice. The bots collapsed whole sections to block them off." Logan turned sharply at the sound of a Reaper's booming tread. The puddled water shook into ripples and furrows from the impact of its tripedal stride. "We can't stay here, that's for certain."

"We need a tripod of our own," Ripley said. She turned toward Rocko, blinking rain water out of her eyes.

"The maintenance panel for a Reaper is on its fucking top," Rocko said. "Can you jump twenty feet straight up?"

"I can't jump that high," Cutter said. "But I can damn sure climb."

Cutter ran to the outer wall as the tripod boomed ever closer.

"Cutter wait!" Logan said, still smarting from Purple Rain's death.

But Cutter ignored him and scampered up the side of the building, using a charred girder as a sort of ladder.

"Come on, Cutter," King shouted. "Just like the course at Benning."

Logan realized that Cutter was deeply angry over Mason's death, and that anger had given him immunity to fear. If only it worked that way for himself. Logan struggled not to give in to grief and despair. He had to lead his men out of this.

Cutter made it up to what would have been the third story of the old stove factory, and balanced on the empty windowsill there. The Reaper thumped into view, its thick leg visible in the ground floor window.

As it stepped farther into the street, it lowered its

chassis so it could shine bright spotlights inside the blasted-out factory. Logan and the Shadowwalkers cringed before the blinding light as the cannons began to spin up.

Cutter leaped from the windowsill, his feet striking the carapace hard. Its rain-slickened surface gave him no purchase, and he slipped to his belly and nearly fell off.

Logan dove behind a collapsed rectangular support beam as the cannons began to fire. The sound, echoing off the blackened walls, was deafening. Bits of mortar and stone rained down on his position as the Reaper swept its line of fire across the factory interior.

Then it abruptly stopped, the lights turning away as it pivoted about to face the way it had come. The cannons fired again, this time turning the advancing line of tracked bots and Chappies into scrap metal.

Logan shouted up at Cutter. "Great job, son."

"Man, that dude's got fast fingers," Cowboy commented. "When Rocko enters the codes, it's like this." He mimed fingers tapping a keypad at an exaggeratedly slow pace.

"I've got him set to escort and protect us, Boss," Cutter shouted down. "Plus, he already took out the other Reaper with a lucky sucker punch."

"Fan fucking tastic." Logan smiled grimly. That was some payback for Purple Rain, at any rate. "Get down!"

When Cutter had clambered down, Logan turned toward his men. "All right, Walkers. We've got a big, bad, bodyguard now. Everyone feel better about our chances? Good. Let's move out."

They headed out into the pouring rain in travel formation, each concentrating on stealth and speed while they let the Reaper handle robot opposition. Cutter, the point man, led their path beneath the semi-sheltering shadow of an elevated highway. All they had to do was follow it and it would take them directly to Forest Park.

Logan's only worry was that other bots would target the Reaper, and thus his team, for a Dessicator air strike. But so far, the bombers seemed to be occupied with Logan's main army far away to the east.

The big Reaper turned its top half about one hundred and eighty degrees and fired at something Logan couldn't see on the upper deck of the elevated highway. An orange fireball tore into the sky, sundering darkness for its brief life span.

Logan almost wished they faced more opposition, so he would have something to occupy him other than Purple Rain's last seconds of life. The way the cloud of debris had engulfed him, choking off air and any hope of escape would haunt Logan to his dying day.

He felt a stab of guilt at the thought that he'd have preferred a different team member to have fallen instead. From time to time, all of his teammates rubbed him the wrong way, even Ripley. Except for Mason. That kid was just a pure and natural soldier, and he fought that way until the end.

No matter what, Logan decided they had to make it out of St. Louis alive. To do otherwise would sully his memory. His death wouldn't be for nothing.

"Opposition at nine o'clock," Chief shouted.

Logan and Fire Team One found what cover they could behind the remnants of derelict vehicles. A nearby car still had a blackened skeleton in the driver's seat, and Logan felt that his team was very close to meeting a similar end.

Bullets riddled their meager cover, and a pickup truck behind Logan exploded into flames when a Skirmisher armed with an RPG turret mount attacked it. Goldie answered with the last of its ammo, enveloping the attacking Skirmisher in flames and rendering it inert.

Bee's Dragoon took down a Chappie with one shot, and Cowboy tossed a grenade into the midst of its fellows. They sprawled about in disarray as it detonated, their gunfire ceasing.

The Reaper tripod continued to match their pace, pivoting around to fire in different directions. Mostly it seemed to concentrate on the unseen foes on the upper deck. Logan didn't know what type of opposition it was vanquishing, but was glad he didn't have to worry about it, either.

At last, they saw the green verdant swath of Forest Park to their relative left. Cowboy sent up a whooping cheer, and Cutter vectored their line for the safety of the trees.

As the Shadowwalkers disappeared one by one into the overgrown edges of Forest Park, Logan turned back just in time to see the tripod take fire from another Reaper up on the higher deck. So, that was what it had been in combat with. The two behemoths turned their powerful weapons on each other, and bit by bit smashed each other into pieces.

He turned away before it was over, sending a silent prayer to the man upstairs for surviving this far.

Logan ran past Goldie, who was navigating the terrain with those spider legs, and joined up with his team in a small copse of trees, so tightly packed it was relatively dry within.

He startled a fox, which dashed off in search of less crowded environs, and took a quick headcount.

Logan looked through the trees. "We still have a ways to go."

In the distance, the boom of explosions echoed above the hiss of rain as the bot army continued its attack.

"Can't believe Purple Rain is gone," Bee said out of nowhere.

"Yeah. Damn, we gave him so much shit." King laughed, but he wiped tears from his eyes. "Now he went and got himself killed. It ain't right. Asshole."

Cutter lifted his gaze to the skies, as if he were addressing Purple Rain in heaven. "Yeah, you hear that you son of a bitch? How dare you take a break from the fighting when we're all stuck here?"

Logan knew that they were venting their communal grief, but he was never able to be cavalier in the face of death. Ripley came to his side and reached for his hand. He gripped it, squeezing tightly.

"Purple Rain was one hell of a soldier," Logan said quietly. "He gave his life to save mine, and that's a debt I can never repay. Well, I reckon there is one way we could help him rest in peace."

"What's that, Boss?" Chief asked softly.

"We can take down this AI once and for all," Logan said coldly. "I'm sick and tired of hiding and always being afraid of the next drone, the next bot wave. They've taken enough from us. They've taken enough." He paused, peering through the trees and back the way they came. "No pursuit. Seems to have quieted down there some."

Cutter nodded. "The loss of one of its server farms should slow communication between the central AI and its armature army. That might be why they haven't started a grid by grid search of the park yet. Plus, we still have our own army providing a diversion. Not to mention our converted forces wreaking havoc."

Logan nodded. "Let's move out. Chief, Fire Team Two is on point. Standard traveling overwatch."

They set out of the copse, grumbling as they entered the pouring rain again. Forest Park had many creeks and rivulets, mostly for drainage purposes. Normally they were quite shallow and thready, but given the heavy rainfall they'd swollen to three times their normal size.

Logan was an experienced campaigner, and knew that even a half-foot deep stream of fast moving water could be deadly, especially on sloping surfaces. So he didn't complain when Cutter led their path along the muddy banks of a swollen, frothy stream until they reached a footbridge overgrown with Ivy.

They grimly stepped over the corpse of someone who'd attempted to hide there. Probably got shot somewhere else and bled out on the bridge, Logan thought. He grabbed the crucifix off the neck and promised himself he'd give it a proper burial. One cross for the entire population of a city. It was something, at least.

They reached a twenty-foot high chain link fence, the border of the Zoo. Logan checked their position on his map, via his goggles.

"All right, we can take a shortcut through the zoo," Logan said.

Cutter lived up to his name and snipped a hole large enough for them to squat through, and soon the team stood inside.

They moved across blacktop pavement that wound its way through the zoo. Logan could see unarmed Chappies moving about in the distance, illuminated by a pool of radiance cast by an overhead street light. Robotic zookeepers?

"Boss, we've got trouble." Cutter had his goggles in telescopic mode, and was peering off in the distance. "From our elevation, I can see the zoo's main entrance. There's a bunch of those gen three bots we fought in the museum gathering out front."

"A bunch?" Logan snapped. "How many is a bunch?"

"I—I don't know, it's hard to tell," Cutter said. "I can't see them all with so many obstructions in the way."

"Guess," Logan demanded.

"Fifty?" Cutter said.

Logan swore under his breath. "Okay, team. Good news is our destination is in the opposite direction."

The Shadowwalkers moved out once more, occasionally skidding on the rain-slickened blacktop.

"Defilers," Doc said quietly.

"What's that?" Logan asked.

"The gen threes," Doc said. "Defilers. That's what I'm naming them. Because of their demonic appearance."

"Who says you get to name the bots?" King asked.

Logan raised a finger to his lips. "Quiet."

They continued the advance, and soon found themselves near a petting zoo, though the animals were cloistered in their stables given the rain.

Logan walked under a massive sculpture of a parrot, and couldn't get over the absurdity of its presence on such a grim night.

They moved on, using bounding overwatch in case the Chappies working in the zoo weren't as unarmed as they seemed. Logan sheltered behind an ivy strewn lemonade stand while Fire Team Two bounded past. So far it had been quiet, and he again sent a prayer to the man upstairs, thanking him for the heavy rain. It might have turned the whole team into a sodden mess, and probably wasn't doing his sinus infection any good, but it had kept the drones off of their backs.

They reached the far side of the zoo without incidence, and Cutter once more broke through the chainlink fence. They reemerged in Forest Park, crossed, and stealthily entered the waiting subway tunnel.

20

The Shadowwalkers switched their goggles to night vision mode and crept along the waterlogged subway tunnel. Twin track lines occasionally emerged from the murky water, unpowered and harmless, but the team still gave them a wide berth.

Logan brought up the rear, followed by Goldie who kept ten yards behind just like another member of the team. It seemed inevitable that the bots would send pursuit down into the light rail tunnels, even if it was to confirm they were empty.

Cutter reached a bend ahead, and raised a fist to signify a halt. He removed his goggles, and held the edge past so the cameras could survey the scene without exposing him. Then he put them back on, and signaled silently. *Tangos.*

He quietly retreated, and gave Logan his goggles. Logan rewound the feed and viewed it. Ahead of them, around the bend, were two light rail cars turned sideways to form a sort of V, the point in their direction. Inside the train cars lurked six gen three Defiler bots.

Logan and the team retreated so they could plan verbally.

"How do you want to handle this, Logan?" Chief asked. "Should we turn back?"

"No, there's no going back." Logan shook his head. "This is the best way out."

"There's only six of them," Rocko said. "We can take them."

Double A shook his head. "They have a choke point. They could hold us off for hours."

"We'd have to rush them," Rocko said.

"That's suicide," Doc exclaimed.

"Let's send in Goldie to break up their line." King nodded toward the bulky mechanized soldier.

"Except Goldie is out of ammo…" Cowboy said.

"Doesn't have to shoot," King said. "All he has to do is trundle forward, with us behind."

"I got an idea," Cowboy said, and proceeded to spill his plan.

Logan pursed his lips. "It's a good idea. The gen three bots probably won't even fire until we show our hand. All right, let's do it."

The Shadowwalkers lined up behind Goldie, the arms of one man on the shoulders of the man ahead of him, and so forth down the single file line. They planned to keep their profile behind Goldie's chassis until it was time to announce their presence.

Goldie trundled forward, its missing segment of tread resulting in a chinking noise every time it slapped around a full revolution. Logan felt a nervous sweat break out on his body. All it would take was for one of them to lose their footing, or cough, or sneeze, and the Defilers would be upon them like stink on shit.

They rounded the bend. He peered through a tiny aperture between Goldie's turret and its main chassis, and saw they were less than ten feet from the train cars.

He gave the hand signal for "now."

Fire Team Two popped out from the left side of Goldie and started firing at the bots. Answering gunfire was immediate and abundant.

Cowboy ran out from the right side and slid on his belly under the train car on that side. His legs disappeared under the car, and Logan ordered Goldie to begin a slow backward trundle. The Walkers backed away as well, taking turns alternating their fire as bullets ricocheted off Goldie's carapace.

Logan counted down the seconds, trying not to speed up his count to match his rapidly thumping heart. Forty. Forty-five. Fifty—

A deafening bang, followed by a puff of smoke and debris, heralded the twin cars lifting off the tracks and slamming into the ceiling. Visibility was nil through the dust cloud that billowed forth, but Logan switched his goggles to gridwork mode so he could still see the outlines of objects.

The train cars were a twisted, burning wreck, and he detected no movement from the Defilers inside.

"Goldie, do us a solid and push what's left of that car out of our way," Logan said.

"Boss." It rolled forward on its busted treads and pushed the burning wreck aside enough for them all to get through. Goldie had suffered much damage in the attack, but still seemed functional.

They continued on their way, using travel formation once they reconnected with Cowboy, who had secretly sought shelter from the grenade blast further up the tunnel. Gradually they felt themselves moving slightly upward on a grade. Logan kept throwing worried glances over his shoulder, expecting pursuit at any moment, but still they remained unmolested in the tunnels.

"I smell the river," Chief announced.

"And I think I see light ahead." Cutter's voice brimmed with optimism. "We made it."

LOGAN and the others rendezvoused with the rear of their army, and gave the order for the bulk of the troops to withdraw. A good two hundred would remain, dug in along the different bridges, to keep the enemy occupied. Meanwhile, the untethered troops inside the city would continue to cause chaos among the enemy ranks, providing a further distraction.

The enemy assailed the retreating troops with its Dessicators, but the machines made good use of their surroundings, taking cover beneath the highway, and the overpasses. They even managed to shoot down a few of the airborne units; the untethered drones also terminated many Dessicators—they intercepted around the passing aircraft and detonated.

When the rain began to fall again, the robot army melted away into the surrounding landscape, and the remaining Dessicators eventually gave up, returning to the city to help deal with the untethered units that remained in and around the bridge area.

Logan pushed the army hard, trying to put enough distance between them and the city. Logan wished they'd been able to recover their ATVs from the MLK bridge. Everyone trudged on, clearly spent, but Logan wouldn't relent, driving his team and the army onward until the banks of the Mississippi were four miles behind them.

The forest was thick here, providing ample cover for him and his army. After marching for half the night, he told Cutter to scope out a decent place to rest. The kid outdid himself, finding a nearly untouched fishing cabin near the placid shores of a tiny lake. They piled inside the two-story structure, which proved to have all the comforts of modern living, even electricity thanks to a generator. The robots meanwhile fanned out among the trees around the lake. An honor guard of fifty Chappies personally enveloped the cabin. Rocko took first watch with them, along with Goldie.

King picked up a photo from the mantle over a large fireplace. It depicted a man in glasses and a red-haired woman who was probably his wife. "Sorry, dude. We wiped our feet and shit."

"He's probably dead, King." Bee collapsed onto the sofa and stretched out. "Dibs."

"You can't call dibs on a whole ass sofa," King snarled.

"Just did." Bee settled in, tipped her hat over her eyes, and was soon snoring away.

No one objected when Logan took the master suite for himself. But he couldn't just fall asleep at will, no matter how tired he was. He wound up sitting on the edge of the bed in his boxers, replaying the moment where Purple Rain was crushed again and again in his mind.

The door opened, and from the footsteps he knew it was Ripley. He felt the bed shift behind him as she clambered onto it. Then her arms encircled him, and she laid her head on his shoulder.

She didn't speak, and neither did he, but Logan felt better. After a time, they wound up lying together on the bed, and he finally drifted off to sleep.

When Logan awakened, he was annoyed to find that he was apparently the last one asleep. He stumbled down the stairs to the den, which now boasted a roaring fire under the mantle.

"Hey, Boss." King saluted him with a bottle of gin. "We picked the lock to the liquor cabinet."

"So I see." Logan accepted a bottle of whiskey from Ripley, and took a seat on the floor near the fire. He gazed into the flames. "There's just something about a crackling fireplace... it's a fitting place for a wake."

"A wake, Boss?" King asked.

"For Purple Rain, Mason Prince, the best damn point man." Logan took a pull on the whiskey bottle and gasped as it burned its way down. He coughed violently. "Damn, been a long time since I had a good Tennessee whiskey."

"Hell yeah, Boss." Bee saluted the air with her bottle of brandy. "Purple Rain was one tough son of a bitch. But he never acted like it, you know? Very humble."

Cowboy plopped down heavily on the sofa next to Bee, spilling a bit of her drink.

"Watch it, meat head," Bee told him.

"Chill out, Bee. I don't got time for you to act all indignant." Cowboy turned toward Logan. "Boss, I got me one of those really good ideas again."

"Oh, lord." Doc shook his head and turned away. He stared out the window in the dark forest and nursed his own private stock of vodka.

Logan frowned, brows knitting together in worry.

"We should all take turns telling a story about Purple Rain." Cowboy looked around the room. Everyone nodded in agreement. "Well huuuu dawgies, I'll go first. Did you know I took Mason to his first titty bar?"

Bee buried her face in a pillow and mumbled. "Because of course that's the story you're going to tell."

Logan laughed at the appropriate times during Cowboy's story, which seemed to involve copious amounts of alcohol, bad decisions, and a place called the "champagne room." But he kept watching Doc. The man seemed lost in himself. He just stared into the fire, and had drained half a bottle of vodka himself.

"All right, all right," Bee said. "Enough of that. Let me tell you about the Mason Prince I knew. Remember when we waited while international court debated whether our warrant on Sheik Agribah was valid or not?"

"Two weeks of paid vacay, baby," King interjected.

"Right," Bee said with a grin. "So remember how dirt ass poor people were in Jakarta? Rain won big at poker that night, like swept the whole damn pot. I suspected he was cheating, and sure enough that fucker was using marked cards."

"Motherfucker." Cowboy burst into laughter. "I wondered how come he got so lucky."

"Right?" Bee said. "So I went and confronted him, told him I'd split the money fifty-fifty to keep my silence—"

"What? You turncoat." Cowboy glared.

Bee shrugged. "Anyway, where was I? Oh yeah, so

I confronted Purple Rain on his cheating, and he said he didn't care if I told on him. He'd already given all the money he had to an orphanage."

"Damn." Ripley whistled. "That's a hell of a gesture."

"Well, he was a hell of a guy." Bee wiped away a tear and thrust her bottle in the air. "This one's for you, Purple Rain. Sorry we fucked with you so damn much."

Bee pounded back the liquor, and everyone else felt compelled to drink as well. One by one, the Walkers told their stories by the fireside of their fallen friend. They laughed, sometimes cried, but when it came to the end, Logan had yet to tell his story.

"It's your turn, Boss." Bee slurred her words badly, having drunk a great deal.

"We should slow down on the booze. Robots could attack at any second…" Logan said, his vision a little blurry.

"Ah, so the fuck what if they do?" Doc tried to drink from his vodka only to find that Cowboy had replaced it with a ketchup bottle. He spat red goo across the room and turned a glare at a guffawing Cowboy. "That shit's not funny, Stetson."

"C'mon, Boss," Double A pressed. "Regale us with your story."

Logan sighed. "All right, you want a goddamn story? I'll give you one. Here's my story. An aging soldier got conked on the back of the head by a big chunk of granite, and when he should have died a much younger man threw the old guy's ass out of the building and died in his place. The end. Ta da."

Logan stormed outside and stood in the darkness next to the vigilant Goldie. "You aren't going to make me emote, are you big guy?"

"Boss," the machine replied.

"That's what I thought." Logan waved at Rocko, who was standing watch on the other side of the cabin, next to a pair of Chappies.

Ripley joined him. Logan was careful not to meet her eye. He stared out across the moonlit waters.

"You going to be all right?" Ripley asked.

"Eventually," he said. "It's going to take a while. A long while."

"We'll never forget him, or what he did," Ripley said, resting a hand across his back.

"Your damn straight we won't," Logan said, and broke into tears. He felt embarrassed. He was a big, tough man. Guys like him weren't supposed to cry.

But Ripley only patted him on the back and held him closer. "It's going to be okay, big guy. We'll get through this."

AFTER SLEEPING OFF THEIR HANGOVERS, the Shadowwalkers left the cabin. They built a little memorial to Purple Rain on the fireplace mantle before they left, and everyone seemed, if not at peace, at least able to muddle through as if they were.

The trek to the rendezvous point was long and arduous. They had agreed not to meet the Progenitor at his hideaway, and instead would join up a good distance away, where they would update each other on how their respective battles went.

One night the Shadowwalkers rested in an auto repair garage, with their army taking cover in the debris of surrounding buildings, and Rocko repaired Goldie's broken tread. Logan had gotten so accustomed to hearing it click he found he missed the noise a little.

Many times he and the army were forced to hide for hours while drones patrolled overhead, even when satellite sweeps were not in effect. Logan knew they had really kicked the hornet's nest this time, and he couldn't say he didn't regret it a little, considering that Purple Rain hadn't made it out.

When they reached the outskirts of the destination forest, the team sent up a little cheer. They'd come this way often enough that it felt familiar to them, when so little else in the sundered and blasted country did.

They discovered upgraded Chappies on guard immediately within. The Chappies stood silently by as the Shadowwalkers passed inside, which Logan figured was as good an invitation as any. The rest of Logan's army remained deployed outside, hiding in an overgrown farmer's field. He caught site of the Progenitors own army, dispersed behind the different tree trunks around him.

When they came upon the Progenitor, he was in a tent he had converted into a workshop. There was little room to move within, because nearly every inch of space was covered by a broken bot. Some of the pieces looked like they belonged to a gen three model.

"Sergeant." He turned about to face him. "You seem dejected. Were you unable to take the St. Louis facility?"

"No. We got it all right." Logan looked about. "How about your mission?"

Marty pursed his lips and peered about the room. "We succeeded in destroying the facilities, yes, but to be honest, I'm not sure we made much of a difference. As far as I can tell, communications between the AI and its minions haven't slowed in the least. I suspect GAIN has already built more backup server farms. Plus, I encountered a new generation of bots. Immune to the untethering. That's not good."

"Yeah, we ran into the same problem," Logan said. "Generation three bots."

Marty nodded. "Very sophisticated. Not a human hand involved in their construction. Marvelous. I managed to snag a few samples for further study." He beckoned toward the wreckages behind him. "In any case, I suspect GAIN will retrofit the older gen bots to be immune at some point as well, probably sooner rather than later. I need to rebuild my army, and I'll have to do so quickly, before it's too late."

"On that subject," Logan began. "If we work together, pool our resources, we can accomplish so much more than we could alone. Look at what we did here, for example. Destroyed three GAIN server facilities, whereas if we'd worked alone, it would have only been one or two." Logan stuck out his hand. "I think we should make our partnership permanent."

Marty stared at his hand, then turned around and went back to welding. "Sorry. Can't accept. As I said, I need to rebuild my army. I'm safer on my own. When you're gone, I will return to my home base, and begin expanding again."

"But—"

"No. No. No." Marty slammed his fist against the metal carapace of a Chappie. "No. You should go now. Please. Just go. I've had enough of working with people. I only work with my machines, going forward. Go."

Logan opened his mouth, closed it, and then shrugged. "You have our coordinates if you ever change your mind."

"I won't be," Marty said.

Logan nodded. "Good luck."

Again, he offered his hand, and this time the Progenitor accepted it.

"And good luck to you as well." Marty jerkily turned about and went back to his welding.

EPILOGUE

Away from the major metropolitan areas, most of the bots Logan and his team encountered were generation one. The Chappies from his army were able to untether them with relative ease, and though Logan hated to slow their return home to the compound, he took pains to collect every bot he could along the way. Especially now, knowing that an upgrade to prevent untethering was likely soon coming down the line.

When the Shadowwalkers traveled by night now, there were hundreds of Chappies moving through the wilderness. If they had to cross terrain the tracked and wheeled vehicles couldn't manage—such as the Skirmishers, smaller Shriekers, and Battlehawks—Rocko and Cutter would plot them a path along paved roads to reconnect with the force on the other side of the obstacle.

Logan often pondered the irony of them working so closely with the bots now. While they were undeniably indispensable, he couldn't trust them completely. That was true of all the bots except for Goldie.

Chief said Goldie had spirit. Rocko and Cutter said it was the interface chip that made him different. Logan was still halfway convinced the Progenitor was playing Cait Sith with them all. In any event, the big bot was part of the team, for better or for worse.

By the time they neared the border of the Talladega forest, their bot army had swollen by another three hundred separate units.

Logan would have traded every single one of them for one Purple Rain, however.

As they neared the compound, Logan noticed that the team seemed to relax, even Doc. He was feeling optimistic himself, a rarity in this day and age.

Cutter, on point, raised a halting hand.

Logan made his way forward.

"Boss," Cutter said.

Logan froze at the sound of Cutter's voice. The note of pure dread weighed down every syllable.

When Logan answered, his voice broke. "Sitrep?"

"It's…it's gone." Cutter sputtered. "It's just gone."

Logan zoomed in on the compound. "What do you mean it's gone?"

But Logan knew the answer. He could see it with his own eyes now.

"The compound, Boss," Cutter said. "The tent city, everything. It's all gone."

The Shadowwalkers filtered across the blast-cratered landscape until they stood in front of the collapsed entrance.

Logan picked up a twisted bit of metal that had been part of their water purifier cistern system. Nearby, Ripley covered her mouth as she stared at the familiar white hard hat of Ditgen.

"We never should have gone to the rest stop."

King shook his head. "They found our stronghold and destroyed it."

"No, King." Cowboy shook his head. "That's not true. If we didn't go and save those folks at the rest stop, then what the hell are we fighting for?"

"How can you be so calm? You lost your wife, man." King shook his head. "We all lost our families."

"I don't believe that." Cowboy crossed his arms over his chest stubbornly. "There were a couple ways out that the missus and I didn't tell y'all about. I suggest we check them."

"We should have sent some of the army back to guard them at the very least," Cutter said. "We were selfish, keeping them with us."

"Without us to babysit the army, there was a good chance they would have been followed," Chief said. "We did the right thing. Listen to Cowboy. There are other exits."

"Oh, bullshit, bullshit, *bullshit*!" They all turned on Doc, whose face was twisted into an enraged grimace. "Bullshit. Everyone's always 'this isn't the end' and 'there's a path to victory' but we all know the truth. We've known it since the first time the bots turned on us."

"Settle down, Doc." Cutter put a hand on Doc's shoulder but it was slapped away.

"Shut the hell up." Doc sneered at the group. "I can't stand any of you. We're fucked. *Fucked.*"

Logan was deeply troubled by the harsh, nigh hysterical tone in his voice, so visceral and raw he was sounding more guttural by the moment.

"Doc, maybe you should take a deep breath and relax," Logan said, stepping toward him. "There might be survivors—"

"So what if there are?" Doc paced back and forth, his hands going to the sides of his head. "So what? Survivors today, corpses tomorrow. We can't win. Every time we think we've got a leg up on the machines, they fucking beat us back down. They killed Gravedigger. Now Purple Rain, too. Just a kid. Killed him…"

Doc sank to his knees and wept. Bee slid down next to him and threw her arms around his kneeling form.

Logan turned to Cowboy. "Let's check this other entrance." He didn't feel there was much more he could do for Doc. The man would either pull it together, or fall apart. Even so, he resolved to speak to him later, when Doc calmed down somewhat.

Weaving in between the trees, Logan and Cowboy made their way around the side of the ridge the compound had been built into. Some of the trees were broken, black and twisted, and here and again they came across evidence of the fire retardant foam they'd encountered before.

"At least the asshole AI didn't burn down the entire forest." Cowboy quipped.

Cowboy led them to a dry gulch, and Logan was about to ask Cowboy how much farther when then came across a yawning chasm in the ground with a rope ladder attached to the side.

"Ha, I knew my girl made it out okay." Cowboy lifted one of the rocks from the gulch floor, and Logan was surprised to find it was hollow. Cowboy pried one end open and took out a handwritten message. His eyes scanned it back and forth, and then he faced Logan with a grin.

"She got out with the families!" He went back to reading, and the smile drained off his face. His jaw worked silently and then he looked up at Logan with anguish in his gaze. "Hanky Bob didn't make it. Neither did Hawkins or Redding." He showed Logan the list.

Logan read it, and sighed, his backpack suddenly feeling ten times as heavy. "So many dead."

"It's not your fault, Boss," Cowboy said.

"Isn't it?" Logan shook his head. "Nope. This one's on me, Cowboy."

"No, it's on the fucking GAIN AI." Cowboy clapped his shoulder. "C'mon, let's go tell the others their families made it." He tried to put on a brave face, but Logan knew he was hurting from the loss of Hanky Bob.

When they returned to the others, they found that Doc had calmed somewhat.

Logan glanced at Bee, who looked uncomfortable.

"I uh, I gave him a sedative," she said.

"Probably the best thing," Logan said. "Gather round, everyone, we've got good news."

Bee's face brightened. "My kids?"

"Safe and sound, in a location only Cowboy and his wife know about," Logan said.

Bee clasped Logan in a joyful hug. When she released him, Logan glanced at his team, and the robot army flanking them.

"All right, people," Logan said. "Things aren't as bleak as they seem. We're still alive, which is something. And we've also dealt the AI one hell of a blow. Unfortunately, it struck back just as hard. But simply because someone knocks us down, doesn't mean we stay down." Logan looked about his unit, at their tired and dirty faces, and broke into a grin. "What I'm looking at right now are the men and women the AI fears the absolute most. And GAIN is right to be afraid of us. We've got a robot army of our own. We're going to rebuild. We're going to recruit. And we're going to do more than just survive. We're going to live. And while we're doing so, we're going to hunt down every last GAIN facility, until we destroy them all."

"Huuuu Dawgies, Boss." Cowboy hooted. "Let's go find my honey."

THANKS FOR READING World War R 2!

I don't like leaving readers hanging, which is why I've decided to publish all three full-length novels in the trilogy at the same time.

That's right, book three is available now! Find out what happens to Logan and his rifle squad without having to wait.

Tap here to continue the adventures in ***World War R 3***

Or click the following link to join my mailing list, where you'll be notified of all new releases.

Join My Mailing List

Thanks again for reading, and I hope to see you soon!

— Isaac

ACKNOWLEDGMENTS

Special thanks to Nicole and Marty Plummer for their "boots on the ground" knowledge.

I'd also like to thank my knowledgeable beta readers and advanced reviewers who helped smooth out the rough edges of the prerelease manuscript: Jerry P., Adam W., Mark P., Myles C., Bryan O., Gary F., Lezza, Spencer, Norman, Chris, and Trudi.

Without you all, this novel would have typos, continuity errors, and excessive lapses in realism. Thank you for helping me make this the best novel possible, and thank you for leaving the early reviews that help new readers find my books.

— Isaac Hooke

ABOUT THE AUTHOR

USA Today bestselling author Isaac Hooke holds a degree in engineering physics, though his more unusual inventions remain fictive at this time. He is an avid hiker, cyclist, and photographer who sometimes resides in Edmonton, Alberta.

Get in touch:
isaachooke.com
isaac@isaachooke.com

Join my VIP Facebook group:
facebook.com/groups/746265619213922

Copyright © 2020 by Isaac Hooke

All rights reserved.

No part of this book may be reproduced in any form or by any electronic or mechanical means, including information storage and retrieval systems, without written permission from the author, except for the use of brief quotations in a book review.

www.IsaacHooke.com

Made in the USA
Coppell, TX
14 September 2022